Guns exploded, the lighter chatter of pistols and the thud of rifles. Off in the distance, behind the church, Will heard galloping horses. The hoofbeats grew louder.

Two running horses raced along the wall of the church. One rider cast a curious shadow. Will fired for the rider's chest, then swung his gun sights to the other and triggered again.

The first man cried and slipped sideways from his saddle. His riderless horse bounded past. The second horseman reined his mount sharply around the corner. Will saw the rider's face as the barrel-chested Mexican aimed a plated pistol. . . . The big sombrero did not hide the jagged blue scar down the Mexican's cheek. Time was frozen for the instant their eyes met. . . . This was Zambrano and Will's chance to end things between them.

Both guns fired at once.

BLOODY SUNDAY

Frederic Bean

FAWCETT GOLD MEDAL • NEW YORK

To Richard S. Wheeler,
for the helping hand

Sale of this book without a front cover may be unauthorized. If this book is coverless, it may have been reported to the publisher as "unsold or destroyed" and neither the author nor the publisher may have received payment for it.

A Fawcett Gold Medal Book
Published by Ballantine Books
Copyright © 1991 by Frederic Bean

All rights reserved under International and Pan-American Copyright Conventions. Published in the United States by Ballantine Books, a division of Random House, Inc., New York, and simultaneously in Canada by Random House of Canada Limited, Toronto.

Library of Congress Catalog Card Number: 91-92210

ISBN 0-449-14779-7

Manufactured in the United States of America

First Edition: January 1992

Chapter One

Twelve-year-old Pedro Morales saw them first as mere silhouettes in the heat waves. The outlines of four horsemen appeared to dance above the white caliche road. He shaded his eyes with a hand and waited. A gust of hot wind swirled powdery dust around him, blowing grit into his eyes. He blinked, but did not take his gaze from the four riders, for his mission was of too great an importance for a mistake to be made. Hadn't the Great One himself sent Pedro to be a lookout on the road from San Antonio?

When there was no doubt about the horsemen, Pedro wheeled from his post to untie the burro. He swung aboard and began whipping the lazy animal with his mesquite switch, for the message he carried must be taken quickly to El Jefe, the chief of the pistoleros. A war was about to be waged in Encinal, and Pedro was sure the streets would run red with blood. He knew he must collect the peso for his labors and then hide quickly, before the terrible Emelio Zambrano and his pistoleros started killing the four men from Texas.

He prodded the reluctant burro into a shuffling trot and hurried toward the Agave Cantina. Little plumes of dust puffed away from the burro's heels, swept eastward by the hot wind. The single street of Encinal was empty, as it had been for almost a week since the arrival of the bandit gang. Gentler folk had stayed away from town when word spread of Zambrano's evil presence. The cantina and the hotel were now home for the Mexican pistoleros. All other forms of commerce had ceased, for a shop owner risked his life when he opened his doors now. Hadn't Benito Sanches been shot sitting in his own bakery, for refusing to give the bandidos sweetbreads without pay?

Pedro hurried the burro even faster with relentless strokes of his whip. He rode past the tiny sheriff's office and glanced through the shattered window, remembering how horribly Ben Wheeler had died when Zambrano and his men rode into town. They had taken the old man outside at gunpoint and shot him in the mouth. Pedro remembered how the old sheriff's head seemed to come apart when the bullet came out the back of his skull. Blood fell like crimson rain on the soft white caliche, forming little coppery circles in the dust that looked like centavos glistening in the sunlight. Maria Diaz had fainted dead away when she saw the blood, and Pedro knew he would never forget the sound of her scream.

"Hurry, lazy donkey!" Pedro shouted, as he rode toward the south end of town where the big adobe cantina sat, half hidden in the sparse shade of windblown mesquites. "The Great One awaits my message, stupid burro, and all you will give me is a trot!"

He rode to the entrance and jumped quickly from the burro's back. His dark brown bare feet scurried over the hardpan to the front door, mindlessly scattering horse droppings near the hitchrails where the bandits' horses stood hipshot, switching flies. Pedro thought nothing of running barefoot through the horse apples, intent upon earning the peso he was promised for the message he carried now.

"They are coming!" he cried as he ran into the cool interior of the adobe. The pungent smells of stale tequila and sweat filled the dark room, mingling oddly with cigarillo smoke. Pedro's eyes would not adjust quickly to the poor light, and at first he could not find El Jefe in the darkness.

Then, seated below a lantern suspended from the thatched roof, Pedro saw the terrible face of Zambrano. Pedro swallowed, and took measured steps toward the bearded giant at a table surrounded by pistoleros. Moving closer, Pedro's steps faltered as the lantern light revealed the ugly purple scar across Zambrano's face. The men were drinking tequila and playing cards. Pedro counted nine as he approached with his straw sombrero in his hands.

"Who is coming?" a deep, rasping voice asked. Zambrano snarled wickedly at the boy, awaiting an answer.

"The Texas Rangers, señor," Pedro replied. "I saw them coming from the north . . . from San Antonio."

Zambrano's eyes widened, and Pedro could see the fires of El Diablo himself burning in the obsidian orbs. "How many?" Zambrano growled.

"Four, señor," Pedro stammered, feeling the heat of the bandit leader's eyes. Pedro quickly bowed his head, remembering suddenly that he was a simple peon who was forbidden to look directly upon the face of anyone who held a higher station, his mother's careful teaching from his earliest childhood memories.

"Only four?" another pistolero asked. Pedro risked a look through his eyelashes. It was the bandit called Juan who asked the question, grinning, as if four were not enough. Juan had been the one to shoot Ben Wheeler in the mouth the day the bandits rode into town. Juan laughed when the old man crumpled to the street with his brains hanging from the hole in the back of his skull.

Zambrano turned a malevolent stare around the table. "Get your guns," he snapped.

All at once men were moving. A chair fell over backward as a pistolero left too quickly. Pedro waited for his peso with folded hands, face to the floor.

"Go home, little boy!" Zambrano snarled, pulling his long pistols from the gun belt around his waist.

Pedro hesitated a moment longer, begging with his eyes for the promised coin. But there was no peso for Pedro. Zambrano began to load his guns.

Captain Will Dobbs hauled back on his reins at the top of a rise. He saw the saddled horses and understood their meaning.

"They're here," he said tiredly, counting the animals.

"I count ten," Carl Tumlinson replied, squinting into the heat haze, cold green eyes moving swiftly.

"We'll be better off on foot," Will remarked, weighing the odds.

"Me an' Leon can come from the back side," Billy Blue said, looking over at Leon Graves, seeking support for his idea.

Leon's hawklike face showed no emotion. Billy had known his partner long enough to read his looks. Leon liked the idea.

A gust of wind fluttered the long duster coats covering the four Rangers. Flat brim hats covered their faces from the sun. Four days of stubble mottled the cheeks of the lawmen. It had been a long, hard ride to make Encinal when the telegram came.

Will opened his coat and drew his Walker Colt to check the loads. Carl busied himself with a shotgun slung from his left shoulder on a leather strap, concealed beneath his duster. The gun was a ten-gauge Greener, sawed off to a mere twenty-six inches. When the Greener went off, the sound could shatter windows. Only Carl among the four was thickset enough to use such a gun in his fist, resting the stock against his hip.

Billy spun the cylinder of his .44/.40, admiring the glint of brass as the shells reflected sunlight. Of the four, he was deadliest at a quick draw, a former bounty hunter and a seasoned veteran of the Confederate cavalry under Hood.

Leon was the only Ranger who did not check his weapons before the ride into Encinal. A check now was needless, for Leon had examined them a dozen times during the hard push across the desert hills of South Texas, to keep his mind occupied. Leon was a silent, brooding man—whipcord thin, with a prominent Adam's apple and aquiline nose—who seemed to take a perverse delight in killing. Only the slightest provocation was required to send him on a killing spree, a fact that had earned him the worst assignment in the service—the Rio Grande border country.

"We'll swing off the road and tie our horses in those

trees," Will said. "I want to talk to the town sheriff before we go in with guns blazin'. Maybe there's more to the story."

"I'm bettin' a pint of whiskey the sheriff's dead," Leon said quietly, surveying the town and its empty street. "Them bandidos have already killed him."

"Ain't nobody movin' around," Carl observed. "They've taken over the place, judgin' by the look of things."

"Just the same, we'll try to find the sheriff first," Will said. "Let's get these horses out of sight."

Will touched a spur to his ewe-necked dun and reined off the wagon ruts. Carl fell in behind on his roan. Billy and Leon rode shoulder to shoulder at the rear. Leon couldn't take his eyes off the collection of buildings below the rise. "I bet those dogshit Mexicans have already killed the sheriff," he said again.

They tied their horses in the shade of low limbs, loosening cinches so the horses could blow. When the chore was finished, Will turned to his men. The wind ruffled his duster about him, outlining his gaunt frame. A shotgun was balanced in his left hand, leaving his right hand free to use the Walker. He pulled his duster open and tucked it behind the butt of his gun.

"Take care of yourselves," he said softly. The eerie cries of the *chichada* locusts drowned out his words. Now there was only the shrill screams of the locusts, and the sighing of the wind as Will led his men toward Encinal.

Billy and Leon broke off when they approached the first squat adobe building, a blacksmith's shop. Leon cradled a Winchester, with his duster pulled back to free his pistol. Billy carried a rusted double-barrel Stevens shotgun, hanging loosely in his left fist. He, too, wore his duster tucked behind his cutaway holster. His right hand dangled beside the gun.

Leon's spurs echoed, then stopped. Billy saw what distracted his partner—a thick diamondback crawled across Leon's path, winding its way among the tree trunks. Leon's face reflected his bad humor over having to pass up the chance to kill the snake. The gunshot would alert the Mexican bandits. Leon toed a rock and kicked it toward the serpent. The rattler coiled quickly and spat its forked tongue, searching for its enemy, sensing the man's body heat as it rattled a deadly warning. Leon grinned when he heard the dry rattling. "I'll come back for you later," he promised.

They stepped wide of the snake and started along the back side of the row of buildings. A dog barked angrily as they approached. Reflexively, Leon swung his Winchester toward the dog and sighted along the barrel. The dog sensed something in the tall stranger. It ceased its barking and slunk away to a garbage pile, clamping its tail between its legs, whimpering.

Will and Carl walked in front of the blacksmith's shop, turning this way and that, alert for the first sign of trouble. Carl wore his duster with one empty sleeve, his left hand closed around the Greener beneath his coat, hidden from view.

Will thumbed back the hammers on his shotgun. The dull click was lost on a gust of wind. Puffs of dust arose from their boot heels as they made their way along the street toward the saddled horses on the south side of town. Encinal was deserted, its stores and shops tightly closed. Will knew something was wrong. It required no talent to see that everyone had gone elsewhere for good reason.

They drew near the sign above the sheriff's office and Will saw the broken window. "Leon was right," he said softly. "It looks like the sheriff has gone out of business . . . probably to a fresh grave."

"I could use a drink," Carl sighed. Beads of sweat ran down his sun-blackened cheeks, mingling with his beard stubble. Carl saw a drink as befitting most any occasion.

They passed an alley between the sheriff's office and a drygoods store. Will halted when he noticed a swarm of flies on a nondescript lump lying in the alley. "Let's have a look."

The body of an old man lay in the shade of an eave above the sheriff's office. The smell of rotting flesh was overpowering. Swarms of green-backed blowflies worked the dead man's exposed skin. A fist-sized knot of maggots squirmed inside a hole in the skull. Will wrinkled his nose when a breath of wind worsened the putrid scent. "He's wearin' a badge. I reckon that's the sheriff."

Carl swung an angry look toward the cantina down the street. "The dirty Meskin bastards are gonna pay," he hissed, clenching his teeth. Will heard the cocking of the Greener beneath Carl's duster. "He was an old man, Will, and I count ten horses."

Will shook his head and turned away from the rotting corpse. The sheriff had been dead for days, judging by the handiwork done by the flies, and no one had risked coming out to bury him. It told Will about the dispositions of the men they were facing.

"Let's go," he said quietly, stepping into the street with his spur rowels rattling.

They passed a small bakery and paused again when Carl noticed that the front door was ajar. Behind a glass cabinet displaying sugar cakes and sweetbreads sat a shriveled Mexican, his head thrown back in an unnatural way over the back of his chair. A dark red stain was crusted on the baker's apron, then down to his lap where the blood had pooled, then dried. Blowflies lifted and circled around the corpse, buzzing, then landing near the dark bullet hole.

"Bastards," Carl groaned, turning away. Carl's eyes came to rest on the cantina again. "Let's kill 'em all," he whispered.

Will searched the shaded ground around the cantina as they trudged down the street again, guns at the ready. Why was there no lookout posted outside?

Will halted when the answer came to him. "They already know we're here, Carl. They'll be waitin' for us when we try to go in."

"I'm already watchin' the windows," Carl replied, biting down around the words. "First gun barrel I see, I'm gonna start killin' Meskins."

Will sighed heavily, figuring how it would go when the shooting started. "Just make sure you shoot the right ones,

Carl. We don't want to take down any locals who get pushed out the door to draw our fire."

Carl grunted. "Sure could use a drink before this starts," he said, starting forward again.

Wind gusted around them, sweeping curls of dust from their boots, flapping their coat tails. The ceaseless cries of the *chichadas* from the prairie brush around Encinal had begun to fray Will's nerves. "Wish those goddamn locusts would shut up for a minute or two," he growled.

A tethered horse stamped its hoof, and the sound sent Carl clawing for his pistol. The sorrel gelding swished its tail at the offending fly and Carl's trigger finger relaxed. He had almost killed a horse, further convincing him that a drink was what he really needed.

"Careful now," Will warned as they drew near the cantina wall. "Spread out, so they don't get both of us with one volley."

Carl turned right, hunkering down with his pistol aimed in front of him. The range was about right, Will guessed, for shots to start from the cantina. He knew he was making a target of himself out in the street, and thought better of it. Changing his direction, he angled across to be behind the saddled horses as he pulled his Colt. Blinding sunlight reflected off the white caliche in his path, crinkling crow's-feet beside his eyes when he squinted to see the dark windows in the adobe wall. His breathing became more difficult, and he could hear the beat of his heart above the incessant cries of the locusts. "Any time now," he said under his breath, feeling his palm grow sweaty around his pistol grips.

A sudden blast of wind blinded him with dust. He crouched quickly when powder blew into his eyes, and in that same instant a gun exploded somewhere in front of him.

Will dove for the ground as the slug whistled over his head. "Damn," he spat, as dust flew into his mouth. Then he heard Carl's pistol bark, off to his right, and suddenly there were so many gunshots that they became a single noise.

Bullets sprayed dust around him, forcing his eyes closed when a spit of caliche freckled his face. He had no target for his Colt and thus forced his trigger finger to halt its reflexive tightening. Guns boomed and frightened horses whickered, churning hooves to worsen the dust as they fought the restraint of tied reins. A horse lunged in front of him, trailing broken latigo, snorting wildly as it charged away from the exploding guns. He understood then that he had been a fool to be so near the horses when the shooting started. Their crazed attempts to flee hampered his vision, and their iron shoes could easily kill him if he were trampled in the melee.

He rolled quickly to one side and came to a crouch, aiming his gun into the churning dust. A muzzle flash appeared in a dark shadow, a window, and Will fired at the finger of orange flame as rapidly as he could.

A muffled cry came from somewhere in front of Will and a body pitched forward from the window opening. A sombrero spun crazily in midair as the man fell underneath it. Will saw blood spittle from the Mexican's mouth as he went down heavily beyond the window, landing in a cloud of billowy dust. Will wasted no time making a run for the cantina wall as speeding lead screamed past his ears. He reached the safety of the wall and took a gasping breath. Before his brain would direct him further, a shadow moved near the cantina door. A swarthy Mexican with bandoleers across his chest stepped around the door frame, leveling a shotgun. Will whirled and fired from the hip—the big Walker bucked in his fist and the Mexican's knees sagged briefly, then he straightened and parted his teeth in a snarl as he aimed again.

Billy opened the thin wooden door with a blast from his shotgun. The planking convulsed and then exploded in tiny fragments. Splintering wood flew skyward, tossed about, becoming sawdust where the buckshot clustered. Before Billy could get his feet moving for a charge through the remnants of the back door, Leon rushed into the swirling kindling and disappeared. "Son of a bitch," Billy shouted, for he had been ready to pour a second barrel of hot buckshot into the opening at the first sign of movement—he had come within a whisker of killing his partner.

Leon's gun boomed as Billy ran inside. He found himself in a kitchen thick with blue gun smoke. A Mexican staggered away from Leon clutching his abdomen with blood-reddened hands, his eyes walled white with pain and fear. Leon slowly raised his pistol to the man's face and pulled the trigger. Billy stood transfixed while the pistolero's face exploded in a pulpy mass, splattering blood and bits of bloody flesh across the adobe wall behind the woodstove. "How'd ya like that, dogshit?" Leon roared, wearing an odd grin as the Mexican slumped against the dried mud, making a red smear as he slid down to the floor.

"You're wastin' bullets, partner," Billy cried as he swung the shotgun toward a doorway into the noisy cantina. The glint of gun metal flashed on the other side of the opening. Billy pulled the second trigger and felt the Stevens slam into his right shoulder.

A blood-curdling scream echoed through the doorway, then a gun thumped to the floor before it came spinning into view. Above the roar of guns thundering in the cantina, the Rangers heard the wounded man scream again. Suddenly he appeared with his palms pressed to his face. Blood poured from his hands, dribbling down his shirtfront. He staggered against the door frame and momentarily regained his footing, then he cried out again and stumbled forward blindly into the uplifted barrel of Leon's gun.

Leon fired. There was a muffled sound and the Mexican's body jerked. One booted foot started backward to catch his fall, but the force of the .44 slug was too much at close range. The man toppled on his back in the doorway, blocking it with his twitching legs.

"They make a pretty sight when they die, don't they?" Leon said, peering down at the fallen man. For years Billy had known that his partner's wagon was one brick shy of a full load, but today it seemed Leon's fascination with killing had grown worse. Billy tossed aside the empty shotgun and pulled his .44/.40 as he crept to the opening. The regular booming of guns was dying down in the cantina, becoming occasional bursts.

"Can't see a damn thing in there," Billy muttered. "Too dark."

"Go in a-shootin'," Leon shouted, shoving Billy aside as he leaped over the body in the doorway.

Leon started firing mechanically, until his Colt clicked empty. Then Billy saw Leon pick up the dead man's pistol, and the blasts resumed. Bullets whined and richocheted off the adobe walls. When Billy peered around the door frame, the gun smoke was so thick he couldn't see the opposite wall. Far more cautious than his partner, he drew back and waited.

Suddenly there was an explosion outside that briefly muted the other guns. Billy smiled inwardly. Carl's ten-gauge had a voice all its own. More pistol shots answered the Greener, until the big shotgun blasted again. The floor seemed to move under Billy's feet until the sound faded away, then there was a noise like the cry of a wounded animal and the sodden, wet thud of a body falling to the floor. "Got the son of a bitch!" he heard Carl yell. Leon and Carl were making a good showing of themselves, Billy thought. He wondered about Captain Dobbs.

The rattle of gunfire sounded outside the cantina, then above the din Billy heard the clatter of horseshoes on hard ground. "Somebody is getting away," he yelled, whirling for a run out the back door.

Billy skidded to a halt in the bright sunlight as a pair of horses galloped away to the south in a cloud of dust. Billy took aim and fired once, knowing the range was too great for his pistol but making the try anyway.

He watched two Mexicans ride off, a big man on a black horse, and a slender fellow firing over his shoulder at the rear. "They're gone," he said to himself. "Hell, let 'em go."

Three more gunshots came from inside and they worried Billy. He turned and ran to offer his help, stumbling through the smoky kitchen with his gun drawn.

At the doorway leading into the main room, he found Leon standing in the swirling gun smoke, walking coolly among the fallen bodies. Leon would kick a stilled form, and if it moved or made a sound, he promptly aimed down with his Colt and put a bullet in the wounded man.

"Jesus, Leon," Billy sighed, turning away from the grisly sight. He stepped carefully around overturned tables and dead pistoleros to a window. "Hey, Carl! Hey, Captain! It's all clear in here," he cried.

"Come on out," Will shouted. "Carl took a bullet. Come lend me a hand."

Billy flinched when he heard another gunshot behind him.

"What was that?" Will asked anxiously from outside.

"Just Leon cleanin' up," Billy replied, unwilling to turn his head to see how Leon did the job. Billy walked slowly to the front door and blinked when the sunlight hit his eyes. He saw Will and Carl in the shade of a nearby mesquite. Billy holstered his gun and started toward them, when he came across the homespun-clad body of a small boy.

"What happened here?" he asked, kneeling down to examine the slender Mexican youth. A pool of blood around the boy's body was covered by a thin layer of dust, turning it milky. The boy was dead from a bullet between his shoulder blades. "They musta had a kid with 'em," Billy said, frowning, for there were faint powder burns around the hole in the soft white fabric. "Shot at mighty close range," he whispered. "Couldn't have been one of us."

Billy saw Carl's wound and the crude bandage Will fashioned from a piece of his shirttail. Carl's face was drenched with beads of sweat as he sat against the tree trunk, wincing. "You okay, Carl?" Billy asked.

"I could damn sure use a drink," Carl replied.

Chapter Two

They came slowly in twos and threes from the little adobe huts and clapboard shacks in the village, approaching the main street timidly at first to inspect the carnage. Most were dressed in homespun, the Mexican goatherders who provided the backbone of Encinal's economy, grazing their herds across the surrounding wasteland. A few wore business attire, and those went quickly to their stores and shops to find out what the bandits left them. Will attended to Carl's wound, watching the townspeople absently until he finished the job. A woman screamed when she found the body of the little boy and threw herself to the ground beside him.

"The boy's mother," Billy replied, squatting in the shade sipping tequila. Carl drank thirstily from the second bottle he brought from the cantina, passing it to Will now and then with obvious reluctance.

Leon came down the street leading their saddled horses. Billy watched his partner approach, idly taking note of the puffs of dust from the horses' hooves in the wind, remembering Leon's grim fascination with the men he killed. "Leon went off back there," Billy remarked. "I never saw him like that before."

Will nodded, glancing up the street. "It's workin' on his brain. I've been meanin' to talk to him about it. One of these days he's liable to go plumb off his noggin and start killin' everything in sight. They say the same thing happens to fellers who work in a slaughterhouse—they get paid for killin' all day long, and the idea gets notched inside their skulls so they can't stop. I'll have a word with Leon. Maybe tomorrow."

Carl dribbled tequila down his chin when he took the bottle from his lips. "He's a damn good Ranger, Will. I'm glad to have him sidin' with us. Ain't nothin' wrong with killin' Meskin bandits when they're shootin' at you first."

"He's startin' to enjoy it," Billy observed quietly.

Carl looked over at Billy. "Nothin' wrong with that."

Will stood up. The wind fluttered his duster about his legs. "The average man wouldn't take this job," he said, watching Leon lead the horses to a water trough in front of the telegraph office. They found the place where the wire had been cut just north of town. The telegraph operator had only sent a part of his message before the line went down, but it was enough to alert headquarters that Mexican bandits had crossed the border to plunder Encinal. What puzzled Will most was why the bandits were still here when they arrived. Why hadn't they ridden back to the safety of the Rio Grande?

Will fingered his handlebar mustache. "Can you ride, Carl?"

"I reckon, if we take along enough tequila."

Will frowned. The two bandits who escaped had to be followed to the border. Only a fool would figure that the pair would not ride hell-bent for Mexico, but it was a part of the job to be certain of it. Encinal was a rough fifty miles north of Laredo. While they were in town they could rest up for a spell and maybe spend some time with the señoritas . . . eat some decent food and sleep a night or two on feather mattresses at the state's expense. "Let's talk to somebody who's in charge around here and then get mounted. We'll have to follow the two that got away. I'll lay odds the tracks lead straight to Laredo. Maybe we can take it easy down there for a day or two."

"Now you're talkin'," Carl remarked, holding the half-drunk bottle up to the sunlight. "I'm a sick man, and I need some time to recover . . . maybe a week before I can ride."

"It's only a flesh wound," Will said dryly. "I've been hurt worse when I stepped on a prickly pear."

Carl stared down at his bloody leg. "It tore my best pair of britches," he said, "and I'm still bleedin', Cap'n. You wouldn't want me to bleed to death, would you?"

Will watched a slightly built woman walk toward them from the general store, a pretty woman, if he could judge at such a distance. The wind blew her soft brown hair around her oval face, and something stirred in Will's groin. He hadn't been with a woman in quite a spell. "You'll live," he told Carl without taking his eyes from the woman. A gust of wind lifted her skirt briefly and he caught a glimpse of slender ankles and well-rounded calves.

"Good afternoon," he said when the woman was in earshot. He pulled off his hat in gentlemanly fashion and did a slight bow.

"Is it over now?" the woman asked hoarsely. She had been crying, and her tears still glistened wetly on her cheeks.

"It's over," Will sighed, admiring the soft lines of her face as he said it. "They're all dead. They won't be giving you folks any more trouble."

The woman looked up at him, tilting her face. Will stood six feet and two, and most women had to crane their necks when he stood too close. "Thank God," she whimpered, and fresh tears streamed from her deep chocolate eyes. "We were sure they would kill us all before they left."

Her remark reminded him of an unanswered question. "Why were they hanging around Encinal so long?"

She shook her head quickly, as if the thought disgusted her. "The boy, Pedro Morales, said he overheard them talking one night in the cantina. Someone was bringing them a wagon full of rifles. The wagon never arrived."

Her answer puzzled him. "We came the San Antonio road and never saw a wagon. Where were the rifles coming from?"

"*Quién sabe?*" she replied. From the look of her, Will judged that she was half Spanish, a not uncommon occurrance along the border, where whites married the only women they could find. Will himself admitted to a liking for Mexican women, although the nature of his job kept him on the move and he'd never found a woman who could tolerate the loneliness of his absences.

"We figured they were common thieves," Will remarked. "The telegraph message got cut off before things were explained."

The woman shaded her eyes to see him clearly. "Then you do not know who they were?" she asked.

Will shrugged. "Got no idea, ma'am."

She swallowed and her face lost some of its color before she spoke. "It was Emelio Zambrano. He is the big one, with the scar on his face."

Will looked at Billy. Billy spread his palms. "Ain't nobody in there looks like him," Billy replied. "I can go look again. Didn't stay long when Leon was finishing 'em off."

Will flashed Billy a look of reproach, for the woman was present and gory details were not needed. "Go have a look," he said. "See if we missed Zambrano in the confusion."

Billy turned on his heel and walked toward the cantina. Will faced the woman again. Down the street people began to gather in small groups to talk about the end to their troubles. "Are you sure about that wagonload of guns?" he asked. Emelio Zambrano was a notorious border bandit who preyed upon cattle herds in northern Coahuila and Texas. The Rangers had long-standing warrants for his arrest, and a fistful of circulars offering rewards from various places along the river.

"It is what the boy said," she whispered.

Will saw her glance at the body of the boy where the woman sobbed pitifully beside him, rocking back and forth on her knees. "Is that the boy?" he asked.

She nodded, and started more tears. "So many are dead now," she sobbed. "Ben Wheeler, and Sanches, and now little Pedro."

"Wheeler was your sheriff?"

She shook her head. "For many years. He was a good man, perhaps too kind to be a sheriff. He was very old. . . ."

Will remembered the rotting corpse and he grimaced. "Who is in charge now . . . now that Wheeler is gone?"

"My father," she replied, fingering tears from her cheeks. "I am Isabella Flowers. My father owns the general store down the street. Come with me. My father is mayor of Encinal."

Will liked the name right off—Isabella was a pretty name to go with the pretty face he saw before him. "Lead the way," he said. "I'll be right back," he said over his shoulder to Carl.

He walked beside Isabella, leaning into the wind as he stole glimpses of her from the corner of his eye. Her soft blue dress clung to her ribs in the wind, revealing the swell of her breasts and her slightly rounded abdomen. He was suddenly conscious of his appearance and thought it best to make mention of it before the wind carried his smell. "Me and my men came as quick as we could when we got the wire. We ain't been near bathwater in a few days, so you'll have to pardon the way we look, and I'd advise against standing downwind."

Unexpectedly, Isabella smiled and he saw rows of perfect white teeth. Her tears were not yet dry, yet she was smiling at him. "I didn't notice," she said. "We are all so very glad that you came. Zambrano threatened to kill anyone who tried to leave Encinal to warn the Rangers. We never knew if our message got through to San Antonio."

"Just enough," Will replied, mounting the steps into the store. Barrels of gardening tools stood on either side of the door, along with washtubs and kegs of nails.

They entered the cooler air of the interior, where rows of shelves laden with goods ran to the back of the adobe. A pink-faced storekeeper was returning bolts of cloth to a shelf behind the front counter. He turned as they walked in, and his face broke into a humorless grin.

"You're the Ranger," he said, sounding relieved. "Mighty glad you men made it. Didn't figure you would. I'm Ben Flowers and this is my store, what's left of it. They took all the guns, the pistols and shotguns and ammunition. I see you've met my daughter."

Will nodded. "Most of the guns will be returned to you. Two of the bandidos got away."

Ben's face darkened. "Was one of them Zambrano?"

Will shook his head. "Sounds like it. My men say there wasn't anyone with a scar on his face among the dead."

"Dios," Ben whispered. "Then he'll be back, and likely with more henchmen. They were expecting rifles from someplace."

"I doubt if he'll come back," Will replied. "We gave them a pretty good dose of lead poisoning."

Ben was not convinced. "You don't know Emelio Zambrano. I figure you only made him madder. We've heard stories about him that I won't tell in front of my daughter, but there's one thing he ain't, and that's scared. Not of anybody."

Will shrugged it off. "We're going after him, soon as my men are ready to ride. One of my boys took a bullet in the leg. The bleeding has stopped, so as soon as he's able, we'll set out on Zambrano's tracks. There's just two of 'em now. The rest will need a proper buryin'. Do you have an undertaker?"

Ben shook his head. "Until last week an undertaker would have starved to death in this town. We never had one. I can round up some help when the goatherds come in for the day. We can get them in the ground, only it won't be very fancy."

"Keep anything you find in their pockets," Will said, "to cover expenses. We'll take four of their horses for spare mounts. Maybe we can ride them down on fresh horses."

Isabella was looking at him and he became uncomfortable. Her unusual beauty made him self-conscious. He closed the front of his duster, hoping it would corral the smell of his unwashed clothing. "We'll be on our way, then. Might be we'll stop by on our way back through, just to see how you folks are getting along."

Isabella's smile widened. "I'd like that," she said.

Will's belly did a curious flip-flop. "So would I," he said

quickly. He doffed his flat brim politely and went for the door. As he closed the door behind him, he saw Isabella smiling at him again.

"Damn," he whispered as his boots hurried down the street. "That is one hell of a pretty lady."

His brief enjoyment ended when he saw Leon in front of the cantina. Leon had pulled the last dead pistolero out front, dragging him by his boots until all eight were arranged in a neat row between the hitch rails. Bloody smears traced the journey of each body from the doorway across the caliche ground to its resting place. It was a gruesome monument to the Rangers' handiwork and entirely unnecessary, for there were women and children about in the street.

He decided against saying anything to Leon. His hands and denims were ripe with fresh blood, and Will saw a strange, faraway look in the Ranger's eyes when his task was complete. Leon stood there, staring down at the bodies. Will would have called the look on Leon's face a look of satisfaction.

"Let's hit our saddles, men," Will said, when he came to Billy and Carl. Carl was standing with the aid of a makeshift crutch, a gnarled mesquite limb, with a fresh bottle of tequila in his fist. "Can you climb in your saddle, Carl?"

"Maybe with a little push," Carl replied. He, too, had been watching Leon arrange the bodies.

The coppery scent of blood reached Will's nostrils on a rush of hot wind. Leon's duster hung from the hitchrail, flapping in the breeze. When Leon noticed the others watching him, he donned his coat and dusted his bloody hands with caliche. "Let's get after them other two," he said.

Will turned away, disgusted by what he saw, and strode to the hitchrail where his dun was tied. He swung tiredly into his saddle and waited for Billy to help Carl aboard his roan. When the four men were mounted, Will reined to the south and rattled his spurs into the dun gelding's ribs.

"I'll be along in a minute," he heard Leon say. "Forgot to do something."

Will didn't turn around to see what Leon had forgotten,

for he guessed it was some other bizarre ritual having to do with the dead Mexicans, and just then Will didn't care to see any more.

A few minutes later, as they left Encinal behind just below the horizon, Will heard a single, distant gunshot.

"What was that?" Will asked, turning back in his saddle.

"Nothin' much," Billy mumbled. "Just a snake Leon saw before the shooting started. He'll be along directly."

An hour before sundown the tracks of the two horses still led due south, toward the border, as Will knew they would all along. The dim wagon road they followed would take them to Laredo. There was little chance that the two bandidos would try to ambush them in the dark, but it would pay to be careful anyway. Billy led a string of four extra horses belonging to the dead bandits. Around midnight they would change saddles and ride the fresh string. If Emelio Zambrano and his surviving pistolero were pushing their horses too hard through the night, there was a chance that Will and his men might catch up at daybreak, or even before, with a bit of luck.

Will led his men into the darkness, thinking about Isabella now and then to pass some time. He couldn't remember seeing a woman as pretty. Will's mind was made up to stop off in Encinal on the way back, just to see what his chances were with her.

Chapter Three

At dawn Will squatted on his haunches above the hoofprints, following them with his eyes down the wagon ruts. Zambrano and his pistolero were mounted on good horses, for the length of their strides had not shortened measurably. "Thoroughbred stock," he said as his gaze lifted to the horizon. "Better'n the horses they left behind. We aren't gaining any ground. Damn the luck."

He stood up in a gust of wind and heard the first *chichada* begin its maddening cry. Only at night was there any peace on the prairie while the locusts slept. Will hated the sound, for it wore away on his nerves and there was no escape from it during the day.

Will took down his canteen and drank a few precious swallows. The horses were gaunt-flanked after a night ride without water. Zambrano's horses would be in no better shape, although by now the two bandits were probably at the river.

"We won't catch them," he said, climbing stiffly into his saddle.

"We can try," Leon insisted, working the muscles in his jaw.

They rode off at a trot, sending telltale swirls of dust skyward. A desert hawk soared above them and screeched a cry along a fast-moving current of air. Before the *chichadas* began their chorus, the men could hear the occasional click of shod hooves on patches of rocky ground, and the rattle of spur rowels, and the clank of curb chains.

An hour past dawn Will stiffened in his saddle, for on the

horizon was a finger of wood smoke. "A campfire," he said, standing in his stirrups for a better look.

"Let's ride!" Leon shouted, pulling his Winchester from its saddleboot.

Before Will could utter a word of caution, Leon was off at a gallop toward the distant smoke. "Damn him," Will muttered, as he drove spurs into the lazy sorrel he rode. "He'll get himself killed sure as snuff makes spit, if he ain't more careful."

They pushed their horses toward the smoke sign, loading shotguns and rifles as they rode. Will frowned when he saw the thick column of smoke clearly, billowing into the growing wind. "Too big to be a campfire," he said, although the others couldn't hear him above the rattle of shod hooves. "I smell trouble."

Leon raced ahead of the other Rangers, spurring his horse recklessly, thumping his heels into the horse's sides. "He could be riding right into a trap," Will said, knowing he had no listeners.

On a rise they saw a smoldering wagon. Leon had already slowed his bay, allowing the others to catch up. West of the road was a campsite in ruins, the burned-out remains of a freight wagon amid piles of discarded trunks and broken furniture. Pieces of clothing clung to thorny mesquite branches, flapping about in the wind. A woman's dress seemed to dance from a low limb, as if it belonged to an invisible maiden whirling to the tune of a violin.

"A family," Will said under his breath, "with the misfortune of camping in Zambrano's path last night." He was dreading what they would find when they rode up to the campsite. A lone buzzard circled lazily overhead, warning that blood had been spilled on the ground below.

Their dust blew over the camp when the horses came to a halt. Scattered luggage and clothing made it hard to look for the bodies, but down in his gut Will knew they would find one . . . perhaps more.

Billy was off his horse quickly east of the burning wagon. "Over here!" he cried, kneeling in a clump of brush.

Will reined toward the spot, burdened by a dull certainty that Billy had found a body. He hurried the sorrel and drew rein at the edge of the brush. Billy held a man's head in his lap, with his canteen to the man's lips. Will was out of his saddle before the sorrel stopped.

"He's hurt bad," Billy said when Will knelt beside them. "Appears he was gutshot."

The man was about forty, clad in remnants of a black broadcloth suit and white shirt. A gaping hole in his abdomen oozed blood down his pants legs, becoming caked brown mud where it mingled with caliche. A blind man could have followed the blood trail where the man had crawled away from his wagon.

The water Billy poured into the man's mouth dribbled down his chin. "He's too far gone to swallow," Billy observed.

Billy's voice seemed to awaken the dying man. He opened his eyes and groaned. "My . . . wife," he whispered weakly. "My daughter."

Billy quizzed Will with a look.

"We haven't found them yet," Will said. "We'll keep looking around. See what you can do for him, Billy. We can't just ride off and leave him here, and he's too weak to travel."

Billy shook his head and tried once more to give the man water, without success. Will stood up and cupped his hands around his mouth so his voice would carry. "There's a woman and a girl out there someplace. Keep looking till you find 'em."

Carl rode in lazy circles with his eyes to the ground, looking for sign. But it was Leon who gave a sharp whistle, pointing down at a pile of dead mesquite limbs. Leon was out of his saddle as Will hurried over to the spot. When Will rounded the dry limbs, his boots faltered, then stopped. His face tightened, then he looked away.

The woman was naked. Her breasts had been sliced off her chest and her throat was cut. She lay in a pool of dark blood that was working with a life of its own as swarms of red ants swam toward the body. The sight reminded Will of a Comanche mutilation. Among the plains tribes only the Comanches left their signature on dead enemies.

"Hell of a sight, ain't it?" Will said as he turned his face upwind to rid his nostrils of the stench.

"Makes a feller glad to git the chance to kill Mexicans," Leon replied tonelessly. "I say we git mounted and go after the dogshit Mexicans who done this to a woman."

Will nodded. "There's a girl around someplace. The feller said he has a daughter. Likely she'll be in the same shape as her mother when we find her. Take a look around, Leon. Right now I ain't got the stomach for it."

Leon stepped in a stirrup and swung his bay. "We oughta be gettin' after them Mexicans," he said over his shoulder as he rode away into the thorny brush.

Will walked back to the wagon and gave the soft ground a cursory look for sign. Booted feet crisscrossed the barren earth so many times, he could not make heads or tails of it.

Billy came toward the wagon, leading his horse and the string of spare mounts. "He's dead," Billy said softly. "Poor bastard must have suffered somethin' awful. You can see where he tried to crawl before his strength played out."

"Save me the details," Will remarked, chewing his lip to keep his belly juices from boiling higher. "They cut that woman to pieces over yonder. Made a hell of a mess."

Billy watched Leon ride in bigger circles around the camp. "Did you find the girl?"

Will shook his head. "Not yet, but I 'spect we will. I wonder how old the child was?"

Billy jerked a thumb over his shoulder. "He was carryin' a tintype . . . had it clutched in his hand when he died. It shows a girl about fourteen, would be my guess. She ain't no little kid."

Carl yelled and waved from a spot south of the camp, not far from the wagon road. "Four horses," he shouted. "They took the wagon team with 'em as spares."

Will nodded. He glanced over at Leon. Why was the body of the girl still missing?

"The tintype shows a pretty girl," Billy said, distracting Will from his tangled thoughts. "Maybe they took her with 'em? She looks pretty enough to make a man want to bed down with her, Will. Maybe they figure to use her for a spell?''

It was a black thought, but one that could not be overlooked. "Could be that's why we can't find her," Will offered. "They took the wagon team. Maybe she's tied on one of the spare horses."

A quarter hour later, suffering Leon's growing impatience, they mounted and started south without finding the girl. Billy carried the tintype of a pretty blond child in his shirt pocket, to make the identification if they found her. They had not buried the girl's father and mother, for the digging would cost them precious time. Now, more than ever, Will wanted to catch up to Emelio Zambrano to make him pay for what they had done to the woman. And there was the young girl who might have to be taken alive from the bandits. Will ground his teeth together, thinking black thoughts as they pushed toward Laredo in a crosswind.

They sighted the main wagon road connecting Laredo with San Antonio two hours later, already thick with traffic dust as the big freighters labored behind teams of oxen and spans of mules. Carl marked the spot with an empty tequila bottle as they sat their horses on high ground to view the empty miles of brushland. The offshoot road they traveled was seldom used, for Encinal had the misfortune to be too far east to profit from the travelers' trade. Such was often the case in this part of Texas—a town was built where water could be found. Encinal's well was both godsend and harbinger of doom, watering the herds of goats as it sentenced the tiny village to isolation.

"How's the leg?" Will asked when Carl uncorked a second jug from his saddlebags.

"Hurts some, but this tequila softens it. I can ride."

Zambrano's tracks were no fresher to Will's experienced eye. He was several hours ahead of them still, and the Rio Grande was little more than an hour away to the south. "We've lost him," Will said. "They'll be across the river by now."

Leon's face tightened as he stared at the empty road in front of them. "We could toss these goddamn badges in the brush and cross after 'em. Twenty a month is all this lousy job pays. I can make more money stealin' chickens."

"Ain't near as much fun killin' chickens, partner," Billy said, joking about it, by the look on his face. "That badge makes it legal for you to shoot Mexicans when the captain gives the order. You'd take this job if there weren't no pay at all."

Leon found no humor in Billy's remark. "I say we cross over and make 'em pay for what they done to that woman. To hell with these badges. It's only a river."

Will sighed. "I've said the same thing a hundred times, man. You spend weeks in a saddle chasin' some owlhoot, and then he rides across three feet of water so you can't touch him. It makes about as much sense as havin' wings on a billygoat, but that's the law and we're sworn to uphold it. Let's get the job done."

Will spurred off down the ruts, thinking about the girl and the terror she must be facing now as a prisoner of the bandits. They would use her, and then slit her throat if she caused too much trouble. Time after time he and his men found defenseless settlers alone in this harsh country, without the slightest idea what they were up against. Easterners came with wagonloads of dreams to seek fertile farms that did not exist, unprepared for marauding bands of Comanches and gangs of armed bandits who preyed upon travelers. So many of them died without leaving a trace, becoming bleached bones scattered by coyotes and wolves, forgotten, nameless, dying needlessly on misguided quests in a land that would never be broken by a plow. And their number was growing.

He tried to push the girl from his mind as the sorrel trotted toward Laredo. He knew he couldn't, but he tried anyway as the distance shortened to the border. If he allowed himself to think about it too long, his belly would tie itself in knots. He was doing a job, he told himself as the faint green line of the Rio Grande appeared in the distance.

They entered the outskirts of Laredo near noon, hats tilted into the gusts of wind to shield their eyes from the dust. The city was a sprawling collection of adobe huts and shops, for here lumber was as precious as smelted gold. Near the center of town a few two-story wooden buildings rose as curiosities above the flat-roofed adobes. Will and his men attracted no attention as they made their way around wagon traffic and donkey carts laden with pottery and woven goods.

"Toughest town in Texas," Will said when Carl rode up beside him. "A blindfolded man can toss a rock in any direction, and the odds are ten to one that the rock will hit a wanted man. I wouldn't want the sheriffing job here, not for a hundred a month, I wouldn't. A man don't live long down here with a tin badge pinned to his chest."

Carl grunted, pouring the last of the tequila down his throat. He was covered with a layer of white dust, as were Will and the others. Their badges were pinned to their shirts underneath the dusters, thus no one would know they were Rangers if they stayed inside their coats. Will meant to ride to the Ranger office, to see Captain Hollaman and tell him about the affair at Encinal. He decided to leave the tintype of the girl with Travis Hollaman before they left town, so he could keep his men on the lookout for her in the unlikely event she showed up alive. They didn't even know the girl's name, so the tintype would be of little help unless there was a piece of luck.

They trotted past busy saloons, already crowded at this early hour. Whores and gamblers plied their trade behind rows of lighted windows. Guitar music and a rare piano beckoned to every weary traveler on the road leading down to the river. Will skirted the slower wagon traffic as they neared the center of town. The office for the Ranger post was a stone's throw from the Rio Grande. Will sighted it and hurried his sorrel, glancing just once across the muddy expanse of water to the Mexican city of Nuevo Laredo. There, probably in one of the cantinas and whorehouses away from the river, a bearded bandit with a scar across his face was teaching a young eastern girl her first lessons in cruelty and terror.

Chapter Four

The four men reined in at a hitchrail beneath a weathered sign designating the Texas Ranger Laredo Post. A short block farther south lay the shallow river crossing into Mexico. Leon glared at the river, as if it somehow offended him personally, as the other men dismounted.

"I'll visit with Captain Hollaman," Will said as he mounted the boardwalk. "You men can wet your whistles across the street at the Last Chance. I'll join you soon as me and Trav get caught up with our gossip."

Carl winced when he put weight on his leg; however, the pain did not keep him from being first to cross the street toward the saloon. Billy handed Will the tintype of the girl and then went quickly behind Carl toward the sound of guitar music accompanying a lilting woman's voice inside the saloon.

Will shouldered through the office door and started out of his duster. A burly stump of a man seated behind a wooden desk grinned when he saw Will's face.

"I'll be damned . . . look what the wind blowed in."

They shook hands as old friends, grinning at each other in the stuffy heat of the room. Captain Hollaman and Will had started out together as rookie Rangers at Fort Mason almost a dozen years earlier, back in wilder times, they both claimed, when the Kwahadie Comanches sizzled the Llano country with their bloody forays.

"Good to see you, Trav," Will said, hanging his duster from a peg, still grinning. "You've gotten fat in your old age. Having an easy time of it in Laredo, I reckon."

Travis pointed to a chair, then he promptly brought a bottle of whiskey forth from a desk drawer, and two smudged shot glasses.

"It's been as quiet as a whore's dream around here, Will," Travis announced, his eye twinkling. "I traded my gun for a striped kitten the other day, so it can eat the rats in my office. How've you been, old friend?"

"Passable," Will sighed, easing down in the chair to pour two shots of whiskey. "Gettin' old, like everybody else. Can't sit a saddle all day like I used to. My damn joints hurt in the morning and it seems like I have to piss all the time."

Travis chuckled, and it seemed to Will that Travis looked much older than he, although they were roughly the same age.

They hoisted their drinks and toasted "Good luck," downing them in a single swallow.

"Smooth as buttermilk," Will gasped, hoping to catch his breath before he ran out of wind.

"What brings you?" Travis asked, when his glass was empty.

"A hell of a mess up in Encinal." Will sighed, remembering. "We had a run-in with Emelio Zambrano and his men."

Travis's face changed, serious now. "How'd it go?"

"We got eight of his pistoleros. Him and one more got away. We trailed 'em here, maybe a couple of hours behind. He'll be over in Nuevo Laredo now. He's got a girl with him, a kid he stole from a family he ran across on the road. Killed the man and woman, and took the girl. I brought along her tintype, so you could keep an eye open for her if she showed up around here. She looks to be maybe fifteen or so, judgin' by the likeness. I figure they are using her mighty hard right about now, if they ain't done it before they got here."

Travis frowned at the tintype, then put it on his desktop. "Lose any men?" he asked softly.

Will shook his head. "One man caught a bullet in the leg. It ain't done much to hinder his thirst . . . he's across the street at the Last Chance, tryin' to drink it dry."

Travis waved a palm, to dismiss the idea. "You were lucky, Will. Emelio is one of the worst rattlesnakes in this country. And damn quick with a gun to boot. Carries two pistols. A bad hombre, my friend. Don't ever turn your back on him."

They poured fresh drinks, and Travis offered Will a cigar. When the matches were struck, they settled back to blow smoke at the ceiling.

"Who'd you bring along?" Travis asked.

Will shook his head sadly before he talked. "New faces this time . . . 'bout the same as the others. Misfits and drifters, mostly. Carl Tumlinson comes from up around Slayton, a big son of a bitch who can piss chunks of ice when the chips are down. Likes a sawed-off shotgun, and he can use it, too. Then there's Billy Blue an' his partner. Blue hails from up near Fort Worth. Quickest draw with a handgun I ever saw."

"I've heard of Blue," Travis said thoughtfully. "If I remember right, he was a paid gun for McGraw a few years ago, when they had all that trouble at Waco. Seems a damn shame to pin a badge on a gent the likes of Billy Blue. He ain't but one shade more honest than the men we're supposed to be after. I reckon that's about all the State of Texas can buy for twenty a month and found."

Will nodded. "Then there's Leon Graves, Blue's partner. He is without a doubt the craziest son of a bitch I ever met. I get pinfeathers on my neck when he's standing behind me. He likes the killing, Trav. He enjoys it. Something ain't quite right betwixt his ears."

Travis gave Will a look of understanding. "I'm no better off with the crew I've got. Curly Tully is off to Las Minas to look into some cattle rustling, but I'll wager the price of a new hat that Curly has found him a woman someplace, and the only cattle he'll be seein' for the next few days will be from a bedroom window. Then headquarters sent me this great big Yankee from Illinois who don't speak a word of Spanish. His name is Harry Oldham, and he gets in roughly three fistfights a week."

"Just like you said," Will remarked dryly, "we're gettin'

all that twenty a month will buy. A good man won't take the job, so it leaves the misfits and saddlebums."

"Ever think about quitting, Will?" Travis asked.

"Every morning, when I'm too stiff to swing a leg over my old saddle. I'd like to settle down . . . if I could find the right woman. You reckon there's a woman anyplace who'd have me?"

Travis wrinkled his nose, grinning. "You'll need to give some consideration to regular bathing, ol' hoss, and maybe a dash of lilac water. I've been lookin' under my desk to see if a polecat snuck in whilst you were opening the door."

Will chuckled, puffing his cigar. "I'm gonna follow your advice just now and find me a bathhouse and a shave. Then I'm liable to go lookin' for a pretty whore, if there's such a thing in your fair town."

"We've got more whores in Laredo than any town west of the Mississippi, ol' hoss. Some of 'em are young, and some ain't quite so young. The more money you've got jingling in your jeans, the younger they get. Drop back by after you get your bath and we'll have a bite to eat. There's a good little café over in Nuevo Laredo with the best beefsteaks you ever ate. Probably stolen beef from over in Texas, but it don't carry a brand, so I eat it every chance I get."

Will downed his drink and came slowly, painfully, to his feet. He'd lost count of the days they spent in a saddle, but it seemed his joints were keeping a tally. He hobbled stiffly to the wall peg and took down his duster, glancing in the piece of mirror near the rifle rack. His bib-front shirt was soiled by sweat stain. Two white circles surrounded his armpits, salty deposits of dried sweat. His denims were faded from too many washings, and when he examined his face, he found gray hairs amid his chin stubble. "A forty-year-old man has got no business doing this job, Trav," Will announced, sleeving into his duster. "It ages a man early . . . before his time."

Travis pushed back his chair and got up with the aid of his desktop. Will noticed the Ranger captain's belly hanging over his front belt loops, hiding them from view. Travis saw Will looking at his stomach; he rubbed it gently with his hands. "I'm due to drop a foal any day now." He chuckled. "The bathhouse is just up the street. I'll see to your horses while you're getting cleaned up. Looks like you brought along some spares, and I'd swear the sorrel is branded Bar Y. That's Tom Baily's outfit, down around Zapata. How'd you come by the sorrel?"

"There's four that belonged to some of Zambrano's bunch. We brought them along, to keep fresh horses under us, thinking we could catch Zambrano."

"Figures. Emelio has probably stolen more livestock on this side of the river than a full tally book. I'll see to their stabling. Tom'll be glad to get the sorrel back."

Will opened the door and clumped out on the boardwalk, slitting his eyes when a gust of wind blew dust in his face. "Damn wind blows down here all the time," he said, buttoning his duster.

"You get used to it," Travis remarked as he swung a careful eye up and down the street. In spite of Travis's apparent good nature, he was a tough peace officer, tolerating no horseplay from his men, while he held a hard line with lawbreakers. It was his toughness that kept him in Laredo, Will knew, for the border-town job was among the worst in the service.

"Who's the local sheriff now?" Will asked, removing his spare shirt and denims from his saddlebags.

"A real dandy this time," Travis groused, making a sour face. "Calls himself Tom Hickok . . . claims he's a relative of Wild Bill's. Wears fancy fringed shirts and carries two nickle-plated pistols. He won't last a month, the way he's carrying on, strutting around town in his fancy getup, talking tough. I figure we'll be having a funeral for him pretty soon . . . maybe before you get finished with your bath."

Will sighted a bathhouse up the street, advertising above one window hot tubs and a shave for a dime. "I wouldn't want the job," he sighed, glancing at the rows of saloons and gambling houses. "If a man hankers to get himself killed, there's easier ways."

"It's a rough town," Travis agreed. Will knew he was reciting personal experience.

"I'll be back when I get the trail dust scrubbed off my hide," Will announced, starting up the street.

A gale of laughter came from the Last Chance Saloon as Will departed for the bathhouse. He looked over his shoulder, then he trudged away from the hitchrail with his clean clothes under his arm.

Will sat in the big iron tub until the water was cool, sporting a clean-shaven chin, smelling of scented soap and hair tonic. An old Mexican woman had trimmed his whiskers and cut his hair while he sat in the tub. "Best dime I ever spent," he grunted as he climbed out of the tub to towel off.

When he was dressed, he risked a look in the mirror. His blue shirt was wrinkled and his clean denims were patched and frayed at the hem where his runover boots met the floor. His flat brim was deeply soiled around the sweatband, drooping low in front to cover his eyes. The waxed ends of his handlebar gave him a darkly sinister look, but the rose-scented hair tonic gave him a sweet smell that helped to offset the appearance of the mustache.

He pinned the badge to his shirt and slapped his duster against the bathhouse wall to rid the garment of its layer of chalky dust. Properly attired, he paid his dime and left the establishment for the short walk down to the Last Chance to check on his men.

He shoved the batwings open and found Carl and Billy seated at a corner table. The saloon was half full, and the faces he saw in the crowd warned that the Last Chance was a good place to stir up trouble. The saloon was a gathering place for hardcases, if he was any judge. Guns were hanging from every hip as Will made his way around the tables to Carl and Billy.

"Have a drink with us, Cap'n," Carl offered. A pair of whiskey bottles in front of the Rangers held only a few fingers of amber liquid.

"Where's Leon?" Will asked, glancing around the room.

"He rode across the river to find him a *puta*," Billy declared. "I figure a whore is just what he needs to take the edge off him, Will. I tried to talk him into stayin', but he said he was in a hurry to soak his rope."

Will's eyebrows knitted. "I hope he stays out of trouble over there. He ain't exactly showed a kindness toward Mexicans, in my experience. He'll be in the wrong place to start a fight."

"Any word about Zambrano at the post?" Carl asked. Carl's voice was thickening from too much whiskey.

"Nothing," Will replied, nudged by a darker worry now. Leon was in Nuevo Laredo, and so perhaps was Emelio Zambrano. Was Leon fool enough to go looking for the bandit on his own?

"Captain Hollaman and I are going over to eat a steak at a little café he knows. Anybody want to ride along?"

Carl shook his head quickly, pouring another drink. Billy waved the idea away with a hand. "We'll stay," Billy said. "Got a lot of catchin' up to do with a bottle first."

Will surveyed the room again before he left the table. The bar along the back wall of the place held cowboys shoulder to shoulder, watching a dark-eyed señorita play a guitar, singing softly. Gamblers sat at tables, hunched over a fistful of cards. The place smelled of barley vapors and agave juice and cigar smoke. Hard faces glanced his way when his eyes stayed too long on a particular spot. It was the sort of place where a lawman could find all the trouble he wanted. "You men watch your backsides," Will remarked. "Carl, you oughta have a doctor look at that leg before you get too drunk to remember there's a hole in it."

Carl grinned crookedly. "I plumb forgot, Cap'n. It's feelin' better now."

Will shrugged and started away from the table. As he passed the end of the bar, he saw a face he thought he recognized, but the man quickly lowered his head. "We've got enough troubles," he told himself, shouldering through the batwings. "No need to go looking for more."

He found Travis giving instructions to a bearlike man in

front of the office. Will saw a star pinned to the big man's vest.

"Will, meet Harry Oldham," Travis began. "Harry's new. I told him where we'd be across the river if he needs me."

Will took an iron-gripped handshake from Harry.

"Pleased to make your acquaintance, Captain Dobbs." Harry grinned. "I've heard a lot about you from Captain Hollaman. He told me when I first hired on with the Rangers that if I could make a lawman half as good as you, sir, then I'd make it. You've got one hell of a mean reputation, Captain."

It was rare that Will had to look up to anyone, but the man who held his handshake towered inches above him. "Don't listen to much of what Trav tells you." Will chuckled. "I'm as gentle as a baby lamb compared to the man you work for. When Trav and I first signed on with the Rangers, Trav could eat live rattlesnakes and never get the bellyache."

Harry hung his thumbs in his gun belt. "That isn't the way Captain Hollaman tells it, sir. He says you're the toughest man he ever met. He tells me and Tully stories about you all the time. Like the time you arrested Tom Spoon singlehanded, or the time Blackjack Ketchum rode into town and you—"

"Enough, Harry," Travis warned, winking at Will. "We'll be over at the little plaza café if you need us."

Travis led the way to a mule-drawn carriage waiting down the boardwalk. A Mexican driver tipped his sombrero as the two men entered the buggy seat beneath a patchwork canopy. "Café Maria," Travis commanded as the creaking carriage started down to the river.

They sat at a tiny table on a veranda overlooking a busy, tree-shaded plaza, empty plates shoved to one side. Will was certain that his shirt would burst from the swelling in his belly when the meal was finished.

The sun lowered to the horizon as their waiter brought them glasses of tequila and cigars. Will had just finished a recounting of the gun battle at Encinal, a story that reminded him of Isabella's pretty smile. "Isabella Flowers is her name," Will remembered. "She's the one who told me that Zambrano was waiting in Encinal for a wagonload of rifles."

"There's a revolution brewing down in Mexico City," Travis declared. "Maybe Zambrano figures to sell guns to the revolutionaries hiding out in the Sierra Madres. Could be he's in cahoots with somebody in Texas who aims to make a fortune selling guns. Zambrano is a bandit and a cutthroat. I can't figure him being in the gun business on his own."

"The wagon was due in Encinal last week, Trav, but it never got there. I'll do a little nosing around on my way back."

"And maybe stick your nose in Isabella Flower's face while you're at it?" Travis asked, winking.

"Maybe," Will sighed. "She's the prettiest woman I ever saw in my life."

"You sound like a schoolboy at a church picnic, Will. I never knew of you taking a shine to proper women, ol' hoss. It ain't your natural way."

"Some folks change," Will remarked, sipping tequila that burned all the way down his neck. The air was cooler now and he was enjoying himself, as full as a tick on a fat dog's back, content for the first time in days.

Later, as they finished their cigars, there was a distant sound that caught Will's attention. "That sounded like gunfire," he said, turning south, toward the sound.

Travis shrugged. "Some vaqueros celebrating a payday. If you tried to count all the gunshots in Nuevo Laredo at night, you could wear down a new pencil to a stub. These are violent people, Will, as you already know. This ain't no place to go for an evening stroll."

"One of my men is over here someplace, the crazy one named Leon. I hope he isn't stirring up a hornet's nest. He's just loco enough to go looking for Zambrano. Maybe we oughta go have a look around."

"We've got no jurisdiction here, Will. The *federales* don't pay any attention to these badges. If your man has gotten himself into any trouble in Mexico, he'll be on his own. We can't help him."

Will struggled with his conscience. Leon Graves was one of his men and thus his responsibility. "Damn," Will hissed around the stump of his cigar, fidgeting. "Let's hire a carriage and drive down that way. I don't feel right about just sittin' here puffing this cigar if one of my men is in trouble."

Travis shook his head and pushed back his chair. "That's just like you, Will Dobbs. I figure you sleep with that badge pinned to your longjohns. Let's go down and hail a buggy."

Chapter Five

The buggy rattled down dark, chugholed streets under the crack of the driver's whip. Will craned his neck to see beyond the buggy horse's ears, for at the end of a lamplit road he saw a crowd gathered. Their driver had followed the echo of gunfire to this part of town, where rows of shabby cantinas sat at the edge of the quiet street, windows alight. The buggy rolled noisily through patches of lantern light and darkness, until the driver hauled back on the reins and the buggy creaked to a stop.

"Down there, Will," Travis said. "Be careful now. We're here unofficially, so keep your gun holstered."

They hurried to the edge of the crowd and found four mounted *federales* in front of a cantina. A fifth horse stood empty-saddled beside the others, glistening with sweat in the lantern light from an open window.

"Let's have a look inside," Will said, pushing his way into the crowd of onlookers. They walked past the waiting soldiers to the front door, and there Will caught the first scent of blood.

Out of habit Will pulled his duster away from his Colt as he entered the building. He heard Travis's footsteps behind him in the silence. The room was in disarray when they entered and the scent of blood grew stronger, wrinkling Will's nostrils. Tables and chairs were overturned across the cantina floor. Will saw a man standing to his left, beneath a lantern globe, golden light playing off the deep blue uniform of a *federale* officer with his pistol drawn. The soldier turned when Will and Travis approached and his gunsights came to rest on Will's belly.

"*Quién es?*" the officer snapped, asking who they were.

"*Capitan* Hollaman," Travis replied quickly. "We heard the shooting . . . we were close by."

The fleshy face of the Mexican soldier hardened. "This no is your affair, Hollaman," he spat in broken English. "This is my side of the river!"

"Agreed," Travis began, spreading his palms. "We heard the shots, Colonel, and saw your men outside."

The colonel's gaze turned to Will, then his eyes fell to Will's gun. "Another Ranger?" he asked, disliking the word when he said it, spitting it out like a foul taste.

"This is Captain Dobbs from San Antonio," Travis replied. "One of his men is in Nuevo Laredo, and he thought he might be in some sort of trouble."

"Ah," the colonel sighed, an unhappy sound. "Perhaps his friend is the one who killed this man?"

The colonel swung the barrel of his gun toward a lump lying on the floor in one corner of the cantina. The light was poor and Will couldn't see the man clearly.

"I'll take a look," Will said softly, stepping around the colonel to view the still form at closer range.

"A *Tejano* cowboy came here only a short time ago," the colonel shouted angrily, watching Will kneel beside the body to pull the dead man over on his back. "This *Tejano* say he know this vaquero is truly a pistolero with Emelio Zambrano, and then this *Tejano* cowboy shoots the poor vaquero in his face! Was this your friend who shoots our humble people like a coward?"

Will examined the bearded face of the dead man. A dark round bullet hole showed powder burns on the man's forehead. Blood oozed from the wound, spilling down the expressionless face, mingling in the thick black beard as it went to the floor in tiny droplets. "I never saw him before," Will said, although he was secretly sure of what happened here. The dead man wore crisscrossed bandoleers heavy with brass cartridges across his chest—he was no simple vaquero as the colonel claimed, and any fool could see it plainly. Was this the pistolero who escaped with Emelio Zambrano? Will hadn't seen the escape from his vantage point, thus he couldn't be sure. Down deep Will knew the bullet at close range was the handiwork of Leon Graves. He would never be able to prove it, yet he knew it just the same. The shooting was proof that Leon was as crazy as a sackful of loons, coming across the river to kill his quarry. It was an act of outright lawlessness, the like of which Will could not tolerate, no matter what the reason. It was enough to prompt him to ask for Leon's badge.

"I've never seen him before." Will sighed, placing the dead man's head gently on the tile floor. "My men wouldn't do such a thing in your country, Colonel. I'm sure of it."

The colonel's dark eyes flashed with anger. "So you say, *Capitan*. My men and I will find this *Tejano* cowboy, if he is still on my side of the river. And if he is, he will hang!"

Will wiped his hands on his pants leg and walked over to Travis. "Let's go. I've seen enough."

Before Will could step around the colonel, the officer's gun came to rest against his stomach. Will's muscles tightened, and for one brief instant his right hand curled toward the butt of his Walker.

"Hear me, *Capitan*!" the colonel cried, leaning closer to Will's face. "If I find out it was one of your men who did this, then you will deal with Colonel Diaz for it! *Andele!*"

Will and Travis left the cantina silently, heads bowed to hide their faces from the crowd around the front door. Travis signaled the buggy.

"We shouldn't have come, ol' hoss," Travis whispered as the buggy rolled toward them. "There are times when it helps to have Diaz's cooperation. Do you figure it was your boy who did the shooting back there?"

"That's the way it looks," Will sighed, pulling himself into the carriage seat. "Diaz knows the dead man ain't a vaquero . . . he had enough rifle shells in those cartridge belts to blow the door off a bank vault. I figure it was the pistolero with Zambrano, all right. Somehow, Leon tracked him down over here. I wonder if Zambrano was with him when the shooting started?"

The carriage rolled away from the cantina, pitching back and forth across the chugholes and ruts. "If Colonel Diaz can prove that a Ranger did the shooting," Travis began, "then we'll have ourselves an incident that'll bring headquarters down around our ears."

Will's jaw tightened. "I'm gonna have to pull Leon's badge, I reckon. He broke the law. I won't stand for it, Trav."

Travis nodded. He understood. "A man has to hold a tight rein on the men in his company, Will. It takes an ornery son of a bitch to want this job, but you can't let 'em make their own rules."

"When I find him, I'll let him tell his side," Will remarked, balling his hands into fists.

The carriage bounced out of the river when the crossing was made, rattling to a halt in front of the Ranger office. Travis paid the driver and sent him on his way while Will listened to the music and laughter inside the Last Chance.

"I'm going over to have a talk with my men," Will said, his cheek muscles working. "Maybe Leon's back by now."

"You want me to tag along and back you up, ol' hoss?" Travis asked.

Will aimed an angry look over his shoulder. "I can handle it," he said, starting across the road.

"See you in the morning, Will. And keep your back to the wall over yonder. It ain't a friendly place toward Rangers."

Will waved and stepped up on the boardwalk, sighting over the batwings before he stepped inside. He found Billy and Carl seated at the same table, with two saloon whores in chairs beside them daintily tipping drinks into their painted mouths. There was no sign of Leon anywhere in the saloon.

Billy looked up as Will approached the table. Carl tried to look up, closing one eye for better focus.

"Howdy, Cap'n," Billy said. "This here's Alice. And over yonder beside Carl is Annie. Girls, meet our captain, Will Dobbs."

Will tipped his hat brim politely, checking the room once more for Leon before he took a chair. "Pleasure's mine, ladies. Have you boys seen Leon around?"

Billy shook his head. "I told you, Cap'n . . . he went across the river to find himself a little señorita. I don't figure we'll see him till sunrise."

Will watched the woman named Alice slide her hand along Billy's thigh, smiling coyly, pretending interest. "Leon may have killed a feller . . . the one who got away with Zambrano. If he shows up, tell him I'll be at the hotel next door. And tell him I want to talk to him."

Billy stiffened in his chair and wiped Alice's hand away from his leg with a swipe of his arm. "You know it was Leon?" he asked, lowering his voice.

Will shook his head. "Can't be sure. I aim to ask him."

Billy swallowed. He wasn't drunk like Carl. He understood the seriousness of Will's concern. "There'll be trouble if Leon went over there and killed a man. I didn't figure he'd be dumb enough to try it."

Will took a deep breath, glancing toward a young woman in a silky red corset and stockings moving toward them between the tables. Dark hair flowed over her creamy shoulders. Her breasts jiggled above the low-cut corset when her high-heeled shoes hit the wooden floor. The woman was smiling at him, even as drinkers at the other tables whistled and catcalled to her when she passed by. Will felt his sap rise in spite of his anger over Leon's bad judgment. The pretty young woman stopped in front of Will, and he forgot everything else. She tilted her head and smiled.

"Hello, cowboy," she whispered huskily. "My name is Rosita. Will you buy me a drink?"

Will felt a flush creep into his cheeks. "Right now I'd buy you a river of whiskey, little Rosita." He glanced quickly around the smoke-filled room. "Crowds make me edgy, darlin'. How about I buy us a bottle or two of the best whiskey they've got and we go get ourselves a room?"

Rosita leaned closer and lowered her voice. "Have you got the price, cowboy?"

"Depends," Will replied. Rosita was the prettiest woman in the place and her price would come high.

"Four dollars, because you are such a handsome cowboy," she whispered. "I take five from the others."

Adding the price of the whiskey, it was a fourth of a Ranger's monthly pay. A captain earned twenty-five a month. Will decided without much deliberation that Rosita would be worth it. "Let's go next door," he said, a warm tingling in his groin.

He bolted upright when the sound awakened him. Blinking to rid his brain of a sleep fog, his face turned quickly to the open window.

"What is wrong, Will?" Rosita asked sleepily, jerked roughly awake by his sudden movements.

"A gunshot," he said, tossing back the bed sheet. He got up and went to the window.

"Don't worry," Rosita whimpered, rubbing tiny knuckles into her eyes. "Men are killed in Laredo most every night, when the drinking turns cowards into brave men. Come back to bed. I was having a wonderful dream . . . that you were a rich cowboy who came to take me away from this miserable place to live on your fine *rancho* in California."

Will stuck his head out the window, gazing toward the river crossing, for he heard the splashing of a horse being hurried in shallow water. Suddenly there were more horses galloping into the shallows on the Mexican side, then a volley of gunshots.

A lone rider spurred a wet horse out of the Rio Grande, its hide glistening. The rider turned and fired over his shoulder at the men crossing behind him. Following the gunshot, a woman screamed and Will saw two riders on the horse galloping toward the Last Chance saloon. Even in the dark he recognized Leon. Behind him, clinging to his ribs, was a blond girl, still screaming as gunshots echoed around her.

Will dove for the bed and hurried into his pants and boots.

"What is wrong, Will?" Rosita cried.

"No time to explain. Keep your head down."

Will buckled on his gun belt as he ran down the stairs. He raced out the hotel door, banging it against a doorstop as he clawed leather and cocked the big Walker in his fist.

Leon wheeled his lathered mount in front of the saloon and gave a shout, "Come out, Billy! I need a hand!"

Will ran for the saloon, trying to see the men in the river. Silhouetted against the lights of Nuevo Laredo, he knew at once the men were *federale* cavalry. Two bright muzzle flashes came from the midst of the galloping soldiers. Leon whirled in the saddle as he swung the girl to the boardwalk in front of the Last Chance, aiming his pistol toward the river.

"Don't shoot, Leon!" Will cried.

Too late, Leon fired into the darkness.

"Son of a bitch," Will hissed, running harder. "Holster that pistol, Ranger! That's an order!"

Leon's face turned quickly at the sound of Will's voice. "I got the girl, Cap'n," he shouted.

The girl had fallen to the boardwalk, and Will could see her torn dress in the light spilling from a nearby window. Suddenly the girl shrieked again as cowboys came shoving and bustling out of the saloon to see about the ruckus.

The mounted *federales* galloped out of the river and came charging toward the Last Chance. Will could make out Colonel Diaz at the front of the group, waving his pistol in the air.

Will swung his gunsights to the soldiers as their horses came to a bounding halt a few yards from Leon. Colonel Diaz had his sights on Leon's chest, and Leon's gun was aimed at Diaz.

"You are under my arrest, *Tejano*!" the colonel cried.

Will stepped into a square of lantern light from a saloon window, leveling his gun at Diaz. "Not on this side of the river he ain't," Will warned.

The four soldiers around the colonel swung their pistols on Will. Men shouted and cursed from the front porch of the saloon, each one trying to get a better view of things. Then slowly the crowd on the porch fell silent and parted away from two men who stood in the shadows, advancing toward the porch rail with drawn guns.

"I say we kill all the Meskin bastards!" Will heard Carl yell. Carl's pistol wavered; he tried to steady it against a porch support.

"Hold on now," Will said, advancing toward Diaz. "We can settle this another way."

The colonel was fuming. "This man shoots up another cantina and robs this woman from a guest's room. I am placing him under my arrest."

"No, you ain't," Will said again. "This man is a Texas Ranger. If he's done any damage over in Mexico, I'll see that it gets paid for, but he ain't going to jail over yonder. He stays here."

"He killed a citizen of Mexico!" Diaz declared hotly. "He is under arrest for the crime."

Will shook his head, grinning crookedly when he thought about the irony of things just now. "A hundred times I've come to that river and turned back, Colonel Diaz. It's the law. Now things have worked out the other way. My Ranger is across and nobody is gonna take him back. The girl was taken prisoner by Emelio Zambrano . . . he killed her family. He's wanted for several murders on this side of the Rio Grande. Ride back over and tell the son of a bitch he can come and try to claim this girl if he thinks he's man enough to get it done. But this Ranger and that little girl are stayin' right where they are."

"I still say we oughta shoot the Meskin bastards," Carl cried in a whiskey-thick voice. "I got the fat one square in my sights just now, Cap'n. You give the order and I'll pull the trigger."

"I can take down a few more," a softer voice said from the shadows beside Carl. Will heard a gun cock. Billy's .44/.40 glinted in the lantern light.

"No need for any shooting," Will warned. "Colonel Diaz, it's my advice that you and your men ride back across that river. You can file an official protest tomorrow morning with Captain Hollaman about the killing. Don't force my hand on it."

The girl whimpered. The woman named Alice parted the men on the porch, bending down to offer the girl comfort. "You dumb jackasses give this child some room," Alice stormed, helping the shivering girl to her feet. "Come inside with me, honey. Looks like somebody gave you a mighty rough time. One of you boys run and fetch Doc Warren. This child is bleeding. She's hurt bad."

The colonel aimed a frosty look at Will. "For now," he said icily, "you have the advantage. Perhaps there will be another time, when we meet again."

Diaz wheeled his horse and led his men back toward the river. Will lowered his Colt and let out a sigh.

Leon holstered his gun and swung down from the saddle. His bay's flanks were heaving. Foamy lather covered the gelding's neck and withers.

"Over here, Leon," Will barked. The crisis with Diaz and his men had passed, and suddenly Will's anger returned.

Leon flipped his bridle reins over a hitchrail and started over to Will. His eyes were downcast and his shoulders slumped.

"It was you who killed that pistolero, wasn't it?" Will snapped, gritting his teeth to hold his temper at bay.

"I was lookin' for the girl," Leon mumbled, toeing the ground with a boot. "The sumbitch went for his gun."

"You broke the law, Ranger," Will hissed. "Take that badge off your shirt and hand it over. You're finished with Company C and that's the end of it. You can draw your pay when you get to San Antone."

"Bein' kinda hard, ain't you, Will?" Leon asked. "I found the girl and brung her back here safe. I damn near got Zambrano, too. He went out a window when I busted down the door to his room, 'cause he had his gun belt slung over a chair and I got to it first."

Will sighed and closed his eyes. "Don't you understand what you did? You broke international law. I've got no choice but to relieve you of duty. There'll be an inquiry. Headquarters is gonna have my hide."

Leon wore a hangdog look as he took the badge from his shirt.

"They cut that woman up like she was a hog at butcherin' time, Will," Leon whispered as he handed Will the badge. "Zambrano had the girl tied to bedposts, with her clothes torn off. It ain't right that a river can allow such things, Cap'n. It just ain't right that a dogshit Mexican can do what he done to that little girl and her family."

Leon's eyes were glazed over curiously. Will shifted his weight to the other foot, fidgeting. While Leon's logic was solid and Will felt the same way, he had ignored the responsibilities of his badge. "It don't change anything," Will sighed. "Come mornin' I'm sending you back to San Antonio to draw your wages."

Billy walked up, glancing at the badge in Will's fist.

"You takin' Leon's badge?" Billy asked.

"Got no choice," Will replied. "I'd do the same to any man in my company who broke the law."

Will turned away and trudged slowly back toward the hotel, then he remembered the girl and turned for the saloon porch, conscious that he was without his shirt before he went inside.

Alice and Annie had taken the girl to a back room. Will found them ministering to her wounds with a cloth and a salve smelling of wintergreen.

"You okay, little lady?" he asked gently, kneeling beside the chair where the girl sat, sniffling back tears.

She nodded her head, but started to cry again. "He hurt me . . . inside," she whimpered.

"Get on out of here, Ranger," Alice scolded. "This is a woman's job right now. Doc Warren will be along shortly."

Will stood up and let out a whistling breath. "If she needs anything—some clothes, or a room at the hotel—I'll stand good for it in the morning. I don't even know her name, come to think of it. Ask her for me, when she feels better."

The girl's body was covered with deep purple bruises, and

the cuts around her wrists and ankles told the story of her misery at the hands of Zambrano. Will shook his head and started for the door.

"My name is Sue," the girl sniffled.

"My name is Will, and these ladies are Alice and Annie. They'll take care of you until the doctor arrives."

Sue nodded. "Tell that man who brung me that I'm grateful," she cried.

Will shook his head and left the room, weighted down by a twinge of conscience. Leon had done the very thing he and the others should have done, had it not been for the damn tin stars pinned to their shirts.

Chapter Six

A commotion outside the saloon puzzled him. Half the tables in the drinking establishment were empty and he could see a crowd through the batwings, men packed tightly on the porch of the Last Chance. Will hurried around the tables, wondering if Colonel Diaz and his men had returned to make another try for Leon.

He elbowed through the throng until he had a view of the street. He found Leon and Billy and Carl, surrounded by men with shotguns. In the dark he had trouble making out who the men were as he pulled his Colt and stepped off the porch, but it was easy to see that the men around his Rangers were not *federales*.

"What's the trouble here?" Will barked. A man in a fringed calico shirt held a shotgun to Leon's throat. Then Will saw the glint of a tin star on the man's shirtfront.

"Put down that gun, stranger," a voice from the group around Leon commanded. Will saw a shotgun aimed his way. "Here's another one of them, Sheriff. I think I heard him say he's their captain."

Will holstered his pistol, remembering something Travis said about the new Laredo sheriff—a dandy, Travis said, by the name of Hickok.

"I'm Captain Will Dobbs. Texas Ranger Company C," Will said as he started toward Sheriff Hickok. "These are my men. No need for the shotguns."

Hickok turned, and Will saw his face in the light from the saloon windows. Blond hair hung past his shoulders. A neatly trimmed mustache and beard adorned his face. Hickok wore a huge ten-gallon hat typical of buffalo hunters from the northwest territories. "Tom Hickok," the sheriff said coldly, needlessly nudging Leon's jaw with the barrels of his shotgun. "I'm placing this man under arrest, and my deputies are making damn sure the other two don't take a hand in it."

"What's the charge?" Will asked softly, trying to hold his temper. Billy had a shotgun held against his spine. Carl swayed drunkenly against an empty hitchrail with a pair of shotguns aimed in his face.

"The charge comes from *Comandante* Diaz over in Nuevo Laredo," Hickok boasted. "Severo, put the handcuffs on him."

A Mexican deputy lowered his shotgun and stepped behind Leon with a pair of manacles. Leon's wrists were bound behind his back while the crowd watched silently.

"Diaz wants this prisoner transferred to his jail," Hickok snarled, finally lowering his shotgun, balancing it in his fist. "Come daylight, that's exactly where he's going. He's charged with murder of a Mexican citizen, in front of a dozen witnesses."

"That ain't the way it's done," Will growled, feeling strangely naked without his shirt and hat. "You're new around here, so I'm told. We don't extradite prisoners to Mexico without a formal request from the governor's office. As an officer of the Texas Rangers, I'm ordering you not to take this man across that river without extradition papers. You can hold him, but you can't take him to Diaz."

Hickok wheeled and stalked over to Will, a set to his mouth. The fringe on his green calico shirt fluttered in the wind. "I don't take orders from nobody around here except the Town Council," he said, staring Will in the eye. A pair of nickle-plated pistols hung from his waist in oiled holsters. "And come to think of it, my prisoner ain't wearing a badge, Captain Dobbs. If he's a lawman, then how come he ain't got a badge like the other two?"

Will swallowed. Billy and Leon were staring at him. "That's an affair between me and one of my Rangers. You're new to this country, Sheriff . . . maybe you aren't familiar with the Rangers. A town sheriff enforces city ordinances. My authority outweighs yours."

Hickok grinned, and Will knew there was no humor behind it. "The authority of these shotguns is what counts, Captain. I've got six deputies with guns aimed at you. I'm taking this prisoner to my jail, and if you or your boys try to stop me, my men have orders to cut you down."

A flash of sudden anger burned white-hot in Will's belly, but he stood his ground and nodded silently.

"Take him to jail," Hickok said over his shoulder, a wicked gleam in his eye. "I'll be along."

Hickok stared at Will, defiant, sure of himself.

"Captain Hollaman and I will see you before first light," Will said evenly. "I'll have an order from a judge for my Ranger's release."

Hickok cocked his head. "We'll see, Captain."

Hickok turned his back on Will, starting off behind the procession taking Leon up the street toward the sheriff's office. Will shook his head when Billy caught his eye, asking silently to pull his gun and go after Leon.

Will wheeled and stalked over to Carl and Billy, lowering his voice. "Go to the stable and get your horses. I want both of you down at that river crossing while I go after Captain Hollaman. I want it understood that nobody takes Leon across that river. If you have to kill Hickok and his men to prevent it, then it's damn sure okay by me."

He saw a hulking shadow move toward them, and recognized Ranger Harry Oldham when he neared the patches of lantern light. "I saw what happened, Captain," Harry declared. "I had my gun ready, just in case. Are you gonna let them arrest one of your men like that?"

Will shook his head. "Go get Captain Hollaman while I get dressed. Tell him what happened. I'll meet you at the office."

Harry shook his head and hurried off, muttering under his breath. When the Ranger was out of earshot, Carl bent over to retrieve his pistol from the dirt beside him. "I say we go bust Leon out of jail right now, Cap'n," Carl whispered, as the crowd on the porch dispersed. "They got the jump on me when my back was turned, and I ain't taking it kindly. Let's go bust Leon out and be done with it . . . I'll let Betsy blow down a few doors."

Will watched the sheriff and his deputies disappear into the darkness, prodding Leon in front of them. "Get saddled and ride down to the river, like I told you. And shoot the first son of a bitch who tries to take Leon across. That's an order."

Will stalked off toward the hotel, gritting his teeth, his hands balled. "We'll meet again, Hickok," he muttered. "This ain't over."

He donned his shirt and duster by lantern light. Rosita was puzzled. "Why do you leave me, Will?" she asked.

"Business. Rangerin' business."

He pulled his hat from a peg and walked to the bed, where he bent to kiss Rosita's mouth. "You're quite a woman, Rosita. Maybe I'll see you again, when I'm a rich cowboy with a *rancho* in California."

She let the sheet fall to her waist and put her arms around his neck. "I'll go with you," she whispered.

He straightened and stormed out of the room, clumping heavily down the stairs.

Passing through the quiet hotel lobby, he took note of the time. "Trav will bust a gut when he sees we woke him up at three in the morning," Will muttered, banging through the door.

The street was quieter now, lanterns extinguished in some of the saloons, their hitchrails empty. Will stalked across to the Ranger office, glancing to the river crossing and the twinkling lights of Nuevo Laredo beyond the slow-moving current. He tried to untangle his thoughts while he slouched in the shadow of the porch.

Leon had been dead wrong to cross the river, and yet he had somehow rescued the girl and brought her back safely. No matter that the laws of Texas forbid any official action in Mexico by a peace officer, Leon had accomplished an objective Will secretly admired. His sworn duty left him no choice—he'd had to take Leon's badge. Yet something deep inside rankled Will. He didn't dare count the number of times he'd almost done the same thing on the banks of the Rio Grande.

Now there was a further entanglement; Hickok was hellbent to send Leon over to Colonel Diaz. "I can't let 'em do it." Will sighed. They would stretch Leon's neck at the end of a rope for saving that little girl's life. Right's right, and wrong is what you feel in your gut sometimes. "It may cost me my badge, but I won't let them take Leon to Diaz."

He heard the click of horseshoes and swung toward the sound. Carl and Billy trotted weary horses down the street from the livery, silhouettes in the shadowy darkness.

The two Rangers pulled up in front of the office. Billy's duster was pulled away from his .44/.40. Carl thumbed open his short-barreled Greener and dropped two shells into the chambers. The big gun clicked ominously in the silence when Carl snapped it shut.

"We're ready, Cap'n," Carl growled. "Just let 'em try and cross with Leon. I'd as soon kill that fancified sheriff as shoot Meskins. He struts around like a goddamn peacock."

"Watch the river," Will said. "Don't start any trouble, but if they come with Leon, I want them stopped. Me and Captain Hollaman will go over to the jail and have a talk with Hickok."

Billy leaned forward in his saddle. "You can count on one thing, Will—Leon ain't goin' to Mexico tonight, not unless he takes the notion on his own."

They reined away from the porch and trotted their horses down to the crossing. Will watched them with a certain satisfaction. They were good men in a tight spot. Sheriff Hickok and his city deputies would have their hands full if they went up against Carl Tumlinson and Billy Blue. And in his own dangerous way, Leon Graves was a good man for the job along the Texas border. Few men survived the rigors of enforcing law and order in this hostile region very long. A bushwhacker's bullet ended many a career before its prime.

Will decided that it took a man who was half crazy, like Leon, to get things done.

Will leaned against the office to wait for Travis and big Harry, wondering how it would go at the jail.

A quarter hour later he heard footsteps. Two men hurried toward the office down a side street. Will's gun hand relaxed.

"Harry filled me in," Travis said, searching Will's face in the bad light. "Where's the girl now?"

Will jerked a thumb over his shoulder. "The Last Chance. A couple of the girls took her to a back room to wait for the doctor. Hickok arrested Leon. He aims to take him over to Diaz at sunrise. I ain't gonna allow it, Trav. There's no extradition order, and it wouldn't make a damn bit of difference if there was. Leon was wrong, but he saved that little girl's life, and I won't let Hickok put his neck in a noose for it. I've taken Leon's badge, but that's as far as I'll let it go. I wanted you along when I talked to Hickok, but so help me, Trav, I'm taking Leon out of that jail and I won't hear of anything else."

Travis let out a whispering sigh. "I knew Hickok would get himself into trouble. I figured somebody'd kill him. Word around town is that Hickok and Diaz are taking bribes to look the other way when a shipment of guns comes across for the revolutionaries around Sabinas. They're in cahoots with somebody up north, according to the stories. It fits with what you heard up in Encinal. Maybe Zambrano was supposed to accompany the rifles down to Sabinas when the wagon arrived. I can't prove a thing I just said, but there's been some whispering going on that Hickok is involved. So far, me and my men haven't run across any shipments of guns."

"It could fit with what we heard in Encinal," Will agreed, glancing at the shadows of Carl and Billy slumped over their horses' withers beside the river. "Hickok, with a badge on his chest, could be mighty helpful."

Travis nodded. "And your boy Leon was getting in the way, trailing Zambrano over in Mexico, gunning for him. I figure Diaz and Hickok hatched up this idea to get Leon out of their hair."

Will shouldered away from the office wall. "I'm taking Leon with me, Trav. I just wanted you to know, before the trouble starts."

Travis shrugged. "Let's go have a talk with Tom Hickok," he said, hoisting his gun belt higher around his waist. "Grab a shotgun, Harry. Hickok's got a handful of deputies. Stay outside and keep the shotgun ready."

Travis turned to Will as Harry unlocked the office. "Where are the rest of your men, Will?"

Will inclined his head toward the river.

Travis blinked, focusing before he grinned. "Insurance. Good idea," he whispered as they started down the boardwalk.

The lights from the jail appeared, two square patches of golden glow cast upon the caliche road. Will saw a deputy, a shotgun cradled in his arm, slouched against the wall in the shadow of a nearby porch.

"Keep him in your sights, Harry," Travis warned over his shoulder, the big Ranger clumping noisily behind them. "Will and I are going in."

"I can just walk over there and bust his face," Harry grumbled.

Travis ignored the remark, for like Will, he was edgy about the upcoming confrontation. "It's a sad state of affairs, ol' hoss, when two branches of the law start fightin' over a prisoner. Let's try to get it done peaceable, if we can."

Travis opened the office door and stepped into a lamplit room where three deputies slouched in chairs. Tom Hickok looked up from his desk. His eyebrows knitted. He glanced around the room at his men when the two Rangers entered his office, then his gaze came to rest on Captain Hollaman.

"I'm not surprised," he said.

Will heard the clatter of iron coming from a door leading to the back of the building. A chain clattered across a wooden floor, moving closer.

"We were just about to transfer a prisoner," Hickok said, a glance over his shoulder.

The clattering grew louder. Leon came hobbling into the front office in leg chains and handcuffs, prodded along by a shotgun in the small of his back in the hands of a Mexican deputy. Leon saw Will, and Will saw a deep purple bruise on Leon's left cheek with a trickle of blood coursing down to his chin.

"I decided not to wait until dawn," Hickok continued. "I guessed there would be some sort of protest from you, Hollaman. Wanted to avoid it."

"Unlock his irons," Will said tonelessly. "He's coming with us."

Hickok shook his head. "He is being taken to Colonel Diaz to stand trial for murder."

The room was suddenly hot. Will took a deep breath. "I said unlock those irons."

Hickok started out of his chair. Will heard a boot scrape behind him—a deputy was moving.

"As commanding peace officer of this Texas Ranger post, I'm ordering this prisoner released to my custody," Travis said quietly. "The laws of the State of Texas prevail in this matter, Sheriff Hickok. Unlock the prisoner, or I'll place you under arrest."

Hickok grinned wickedly, enjoying things. "The law of the gun prevails here, Hollaman. Turn around and have a look."

A shotgun clicked once, then another. Will didn't need to turn around to know the three deputies had them covered.

"You're making a big mistake, Hickok," Will warned.

"Maybe," the sheriff sighed. "I'm doing it anyway."

Travis looked over at Will, pinching his brow. "I reckon they've got us, Will," he said quickly, before Will could utter a protest. "If we hurry back to my office, we can get off a wire to the capital about this. I'll see Judge Green and we can get a warrant for Sheriff Hickok's arrest."

Will's jaw tightened, until he caught a wink from Travis that had him puzzled. "Come on, Will, let's get going. We can watch the sheriff and his men ride across the river, so we know my official order has been ignored."

"You're being sensible," Hickok said.

Travis caught Will by the arm and led him out, past the three glowering deputies cradling shotguns. Will pulled his arm away when they were outside. "I never backed down from nobody in my life, Trav."

"They had us cold, Will," Travis whispered, hurrying down the boardwalk to the shadow where Harry waited. "We'll stop them at the river, where your men are mounted. Out in the open the odds don't stack up against us. You always were too damn hot-headed, Will. You were lucky a damn Comanche didn't lift your scalp back at Fort Mason, charging them like you did."

Harry fell in behind them as they made their way back to the river. "What happened, Captain?" he asked.

"Nothing yet, Harry," Travis replied. "But I figure you're about to get your chance to do a little fighting."

Travis ducked in the office and hurriedly pulled shotguns from a wall rack, handing one to Will. "Check the loads. Double O's are on the top shelf."

They loaded and doused the lantern. Will ran out on the dark porch, waving a signal to Carl and Billy. One rider waved back and the two horses parted, halting on either side of the crossing.

"Get across the street, Harry," Travis snapped. "In the alley next to the Last Chance. Don't fire until I give the order . . . unless they start shooting first."

Harry lumbered across the empty street and disappeared in the alley shadows. Will and Travis went to the side of the office and waited, listening for the sounds of moving horses.

Chapter Seven

An eternity of waiting. Will's palms grew wet on the gun stock, straining to hear the first footfall. "Maybe they went downriver," he suggested. "It's been too long. Something don't seem right."

Travis swung a look east. "I'll run down and have a look. You keep an eye open here."

Travis was gone before Will could protest. He listened to the soft patter of boots until they faded. "Damn," Will hissed, growing edgier by the minute.

A shout shattered the silence. Will saw Billy spur his horse to a lope down the riverbank. Carl dug his spurs into the roan and soon he was out of sight. Will cursed silently and broke into a run toward the river.

A shotgun roared, followed by a yell. Then guns boomed in unison, the bark of pistols and the heavy discharge of shotgun blasts, echoing off the buildings on Main Street. Will ran as hard as he could and rounded the last adobe above the river in an all-out charge. Guns thundered in the darkness downstream.

He ran along the water's edge, and now he could see horses lunging back and forth in the shallows. He scented gunpowder, and by the light from the stars he could make out the dim outlines of the riders. Muzzles flashed. Men cried and cursed in the darkness. Will was too far from the men to find a target he recognized, unwilling to risk a careless shot that might endanger his men.

Suddenly the Greener gave off its unmistakable roar and a rider was torn from the back of his horse. The man screamed as he flew sideways out of the saddle, then his scream ended as he fell below the surface of the river. "Got the son of a bitch!" he heard Carl yell.

The Greener thundered again. A horse whickered and fell on its side, thrashing its hooves, churning the inky water to white foam. Will saw the rider spill off the horse's rump, landing with a soundless splash as the guns blasted back and forth.

A shotgun roared from the riverbank. Will ran headlong to join Travis at the river's edge, his breath whistling through his nostrils. Travis aimed again at a running horse. The blast rocked Travis back a half step. The rider slumped over his horse's neck. A gun barrel glinted in the starlight and a finger of bright flame came from the rider's pistol. Will stumbled to a halt and took quick aim as the galloping horse charged toward him. When the shotgun steadied, Will pulled a trigger. The report echoed as the gun slammed into Will's shoulder. A shadow spun crazily from the horse's back, twirling in midair, arms and legs askew. The running horse snorted and shied from the gunshot, kicking foamy spray from its hooves. The rider fell upon the surface of the river disjointedly and sank out of sight, making bubbles.

A man staggered to his feet in the shallows and threw up his hands. "Don't shoot!" he cried above the bang of guns. He was cut down before the last word left his lips by a bellowing blast from the Greener. Carl charged back into the fight with the shotgun in one fist and his pistol in the other, spurring his mount recklessly into the midst of the fray.

A lunging horse distracted Will—he recognized Billy's hat outlined against the lights of Nuevo Laredo. A hatless rider clung to Billy's back as the horse charged away from the firefight. "He got Leon," Will shouted, trying to draw Carl's attention. But Carl could not hear him, firing his Colt at the shadow of a fleeing horseman, spurring his roan in relentless pursuit. Three shots echoed from Carl's pistol before the rider rolled, ball-like, off the galloping horse's rump, arms flailing. The body landed on the soft riverbank sand with a dull thump and went still.

One rider spurred off down the riverbank, firing once over his shoulder. The bullet skittered harmlessly across the water, cutting a foamy furrow, gurgling softly.

Carl jerked his roan around roughly, his face sweeping back and forth for another target, holding a tight rein on his frightened mount. Riderless horses trotted out of the river, snorting, ears flicking back and forth, awaiting the next loud noise. Will trained the shotgun on the river and searched the darkness. There were no survivors of the river fight to shoot at. A body floated away from the river's edge, caught briefly in an eddy, swirling before it was carried southeast by the current. In place of the roar of the guns there was an eerie silence now. A filmy cloud of blue gun smoke layered over the dark water, caught between the men and the lights of the Mexican city on the opposite bank. The wind carried the smoke away in rolling curls.

"One of the bastards got away," Carl shouted. "You want me to go after him, Cap'n?"

"Let him go," Will sighed, balancing the shotgun in one hand. "Billy has Leon. We got what we wanted."

Leon was off the rump of Billy's horse near the river crossing. Will saw Harry standing beside them, his shotgun ready if more trouble came. Then Will heard Travis approach along the riverbank behind him.

"They were trying to slip across downstream, Will," Travis said. "Hickok got away . . . the yellow bastard took off when he saw that his men were licked. There's gonna be one hell of a stink over this, ol' hoss. I'll head over to Judge Green's so I can start explaining things. I'd imagine headquarters will call you in when they get the word. You'll have a lot of tall talking to do. I'll send in my report, to back your story up. But I still figure they'll read your pedigree to you a time or two."

Curious drinkers gathered on the front porch of the Last Chance, drawn outside by the gunfire. Men clustered, pointing to the river. Will shook his head and sighed. "You're right, Trav. Headquarters will investigate everything. I figure this will cost me my badge, but I couldn't let Hickok stretch

Leon's neck over in Mexico. I plain couldn't let 'em do it. I reckon when a feller gets too soft to do his job, he oughta quit. Leon was wrong, going over to get the girl, but I had to back his play . . . couldn't stomach it any other way."

Travis shrugged and stared across the river. "I would have done the same thing, most likely. There's nothing that special about a twenty-five-dollar-a-month job anyways. You've got one hell of a record with the Rangers, Will. I don't figure they'll ask for your badge. Maybe slap your wrists a time or two."

They heard Carl's horse trotting up the river. Will swung toward the sound.

"We showed 'em a thing or two, Cap'n," Carl said, pulling down on his roan. "I tried to kill that fancified sheriff . . . couldn't find him in the dark. Hell, Will, he ain't no lawman. He's a damn gunslinger with a tin badge, struttin' around like a peacock with his feathers stuck out. Something don't ring true about him. Why was he in such a big hurry to get Leon over to the *federales*?"

"Maybe because Hickok is involved in gun-smuggling," Will replied. "He may be tied to the wagonload of guns Zambrano was waiting for up in Encinal."

Carl digested the thought. "Wonder what happened to that wagon?" he asked.

Will watched Billy and Leon start toward them. "Maybe we oughta look into it on our way back . . . do a little scouting around for sign of that shipment of rifles."

Leon was soaked to the skin, his wrists bound in manacles. He grinned sheepishly when he got to Will. "Sure glad you gents came along when you did. I was headed to a necktie party."

Will's shoulders dropped. "None of this would have happened if you'd stayed where you belonged," he said.

Leon aimed a thumb toward Mexico. "And that little bitty girl would still be over yonder, hog-tied to that bed. Maybe she'd even be dead by now, Cap'n. It didn't seem right to ride off an' leave her, not after what Zambrano done to her maw and paw. I done it Capt'n . . . just like you said. I killed that dogshit Mexican when he went for his gun, and I damn sure tried to kill Zambrano. Main thing I set out to do was get that little girl back."

"Leon damn sure got it done, too," Billy remarked softly. "I say you oughta give Leon back his badge and make him a full-fledged Ranger. Ain't many men got the backbone to do what Leon did, and he done it on account of that kid."

A few curious onlookers came down the riverbank. "Who was doing all the shooting?" someone asked from the darkness.

Will started back to the hotel without offering a reply, events weighing heavily on his shoulders. Travis caught up and took the shotgun from Will's hand. "I'll head over to Judge Green's and tell him what happened. See you at the office. Ain't long till dawn. We'll boil a pot of coffee."

Will nodded. "Me and the boys are headed to Hickok's office to get the keys to Leon's handcuffs. We won't be long."

They walked up the silent street, past the saloon and its darkened windows. An hour before dawn Laredo was finally asleep, its streets empty.

At the lamplit office Will approached carefully, but found no one inside. He walked to the desk while the others waited outside, rummaging through desk drawers in search of the key.

At the back of a bottom desk drawer Will discovered a curious envelope, a letter addressed to Tom Hickok folded and wilted by long passage in a pants pocket. The envelope bore a Spanish word *Manifesto*, in one corner. Will frowned and thumbed it open.

He peered down at a wrinkled order for four hundred Winchester Repeating rifles from a firm in Kansas City, Stanford Arms. On the following line was an order for ten crates of .44/.44 ammunition and a bold checkmark. "The wagonload of rifles," he whispered, "the guns headed for Encinal."

He stuck the letter in his shirt pocket and closed the desk drawer. "Got you, Hickok," he said softly. "You're a goddamn gun-runner, or a paid accomplice." Maybe Hickok was only looking the other way when they come across, but he was up to his damn neck in the gun-smuggling business. No wonder he wanted Leon off Emelio Zambrano's tail— Zambrano escorted the guns across the river.

Things were falling into place . . . finally beginning to make some sense. Diaz warned Hickok that a Ranger was getting too close to Zambrano in Nuevo Laredo, most likely as Zambrano was trying to round up more men to return for the guns. Diaz could have sent a messenger across to Hickok after Leon shot the pistolero at the cantina. Hadn't Diaz said that the *Tejano* claimed the dead man was with Zambrano, when Will and Travis came to the cantina? It was starting to fit like a glove.

Will found the keys in another drawer and hurried outside to remove the cuffs. "I found something," Will said, as Billy took the irons off Leon's wrists. "Hickok is involved with the rifles headed for Encinal. I found a manifest in his desk drawer. Let's get back to the office so I can show Captain Hollaman what I found."

Travis frowned while he read the manifest from Kansas City. Coffee bubbled on the potbelly in a corner of the room, smelling stronger, reminding Will that his belly was empty.

"I need to show this to Judge Green," Travis remarked. "It appears our new sheriff dabbles in smuggled guns. This manifest says that the rifles were sold to Porfirio Ortega of Saltillo, Mexico. Stanford Arms is partly to blame here . . . as gun dealers, they know about the ban on selling guns to anyone in Mexico without the Mexican government's approval. There's no seal on this document from Mexico City, so it's safe to assume these rifles are headed to the revolutionaries in the mountains."

Will grunted, fidgeting in his seat. "What did the judge say about Leon and the shooting over in Nuevo Laredo?"

Travis folded the manifest and stuck it in his shirt. "He'll hold an inquest and invite Colonel Diaz to file a formal complaint. It could take months. I told the judge that you had suspended the Ranger. He seemed satisfied. The fight with

Hickok and his deputies is another matter. Some of the men who were killed have families who'll raise a stink. There will be a hearing before the city attorney, to see if charges can be filed against the Texas Rangers who took part in it. That includes me. When I show Judge Green this manifest for the rifles, I think it will help explain Hickok's actions. I don't look for Hickok to show his face again in Laredo after last night. I figure he's tucked tail and run."

"Maybe," Will said, "or maybe he'll ride north to find out what happened to the guns. I figure that's where me and my men will ride—back to Encinal, just to nose around."

Travis nodded, pouring steaming coffee into tin cups. A streak of sunlight lit the east window of the office as dawn crept into the brightening sky. "Send a wire if you find anything. I reckon the line is fixed by now."

"I'll let you know," Will said, blowing to cool the contents of his cup. "I wonder who was bringing the wagon down from Kansas City?"

"Armed guards, if I had to take a guess. The shipment's too valuable and it would be discovered as contraband, guns without proper clearance on the way to Mexico by regular freight wagons."

"Hired guns," Will said absently, thinking out loud. "They wouldn't risk traveling the usual routes. Too risky. Maybe that's an explanation for the delay—traveling cross-country. I reckon we'll ride north and have a look for ourselves."

"Keep looking over your shoulder, Will. Zambrano may be back with more pistoleros, looking for the same wagon. You could get caught in the cross-fire."

"Figures," Will sighed, thinking black thoughts. "Will you see that the girl gets sent to the closest relatives, Trav? It would be too dangerous, taking her along with us. Besides, I figure the doctor needs to take care of her for a few days. I only hope the child has some family someplace. . . ."

"I'll see to it," Travis said, adding a splash of whiskey to their morning coffee. "You keep an eye open for Zambrano and find that load of rifles. I'll handle things here."

Chapter Eight

They pushed their horses into the cool of evening. Purple shadows fell away from spiked yucca and agave, softening the spines of the pear cactus and the needlelike thorns of the mesquite limbs swaying in the wind. The *chichadas* muted their cries with the coming of dusk, enabling the men to hear the dry rattle of mesquite beans on nearby trees. Powdery dust arose from the horses' heels as they trotted northward. Wind swept the dust ahead and slightly east of the Encinal road. Will's dun coughed, lowering its head to rid its muzzle of white chalk. The irregular click of iron broke the stillness when a horse trotted over rocky ground. An owl hooted from the west, its voice carried on the wind.

"It's mighty dry," Carl observed, scanning the gentle hills in their path. "This country ain't fit for nothin' but lizards and snakes."

"Shut up, Carl," Billy protested. "You're makin' me thirsty."

"I could use a drink myself," Carl replied predictably. It wasn't water Carl had in mind.

"Encinal ain't far," Will said. "You can wet your whistles in a couple hours."

"You gonna look for that pretty lady when we get there?" Carl asked.

Will had been thinking about Isabella for the last few miles, remembering her beautiful face and the crinkled corners of her easy smile. "Maybe." He shrugged, a form of denial. It was none of Carl's business what he did with his free time. Isabella's big chocolate eyes danced before him, seeming to float on the horizon when he thought about her. "I might," he said, knowing wild horses couldn't keep him from an attempt to share her company when they reached Encinal.

He thought about Leon then . . . strangely enough, for Leon rode shamefaced at the rear without a word to the others, and Will had almost forgotten that he rode along. Leon's badge rested in Will's pocket, and Will supposed that it explained Leon's silence. He was not a Ranger now, and that fact set him apart.

Leon's actions still weighed heavily on Will's mind. The plain truth was that Will found it harder and harder to place blame on Leon for what he had done. The girl was back safe, and a murdering pistolero was in a grave in Nuevo Laredo, not really an undesirable outcome when it was viewed in the right light. A darker truth was that Will had come within a whisker of performing the same unlawful act countless times as he sat his horse on the banks of the Rio Grande, sighting along a set of tracks that made the crossing into Mexico. Once, hot on the trail of two outlaws who had outridden him to the border above Piedras Negras, Will sat his saddle and gripped the saddlehorn until his fingers hurt when he saw the silhouettes of the pair on a distant hilltop. He imagined they were laughing at him, for a three-foot depth of muddy water halted his pursuit as surely as a lariat afixed to a stump. He was forced to sit there as the outlaws rode off the rise, and unless his eyes played tricks on him, he was sure one of the men waved to him before he rode out of sight.

"All of this on account of a river," Will said, struggling with his conscience. He was sworn to uphold the laws of Texas, and the law plainly kept him from entering Mexico. No reason was good enough to cross after a lawbreaker, and that would be the same speech Major Peoples would read to him when headquarters inquired about the incident. Nothing Will said would make any difference to the major—his rules were always worded in plain English and there was never any middle ground. Leon Graves was finished as a Texas Ranger. Will was a man without choices.

Evening became dusk. The air breathed cooler from the

southwest and the cries of the locusts ceased. Only the dust remained, always in front of them as trotting hooves pounded the dry caliche. At night the dust reminded Will of frosty vapor on a cold morning when it curled away from the horses. The dust was always a telltale sign of man's passing through this desolate wasteland. No living thing could move about in South Texas without leaving dust sign above its travels. The floor-length duster coats kept Will and his men from turning the same chalky white as the land they rode through. In spite of the heat from added clothing, experienced men wore the dusters, summer and winter.

Full dark came, and the sky brightened with twinkling stars. The four rode silently toward Encinal, weapons slung from saddles and hidden beneath their coats. The clank of iron sent night birds skittering from branches in their path as the men followed the dim wagon ruts north.

The lights of the village twinkled in the distance. Will saw them and stood in his stirrups for a better look.

"There's Encinal," Carl muttered, "and a bottle of tequila with my name painted on it. Maybe two of 'em. My throat's gone mighty dry."

"We ride in careful," Will warned, settling again on the dun's back. "Keep your eyes peeled for a freight wagon."

He heard a horse hurrying to ride alongside. When he turned for a look, he found Leon trotting past the others.

"How about it, Cap'n?" Leon asked quietly. "If there's any trouble, you want me to lend you a hand?"

"Not officially," Will replied. "The three of us can handle it if trouble starts."

Will's words stung Leon like a lash across his face. He shook his head and fell back, ducking his head.

He'll never understand, Will told himself. Leon figured he was being too hard on him. Leon ain't cut out to be a lawman. A soldier, maybe. There's other things to being a lawman besides killing.

Will argued with himself over the dwindling miles to Encinal, trotting through the darkness while common sense debated logic over Leon's guilt or innocence.

On a crest above the town they rode past a tiny graveyard surrounded by a sagging picket fence fashioned from mesquite limbs. A mound of fresh earth, then another, reflected starlight. A crude plank marker bore Ben Wheeler's name. A second, that of Benito Sanches. Beside it lay the grave of the boy. A handful of pink cactus blooms rested against the marker, pale in the faint light. The graveyard was a reminder of the grisly chore they performed earlier in the day, at the burned-out wagon. Fighting away the hungry vultures, they had grubbed out shallow graves for the man and woman . . . what was left of them after the feeding by coyotes and buzzards and swarms of red ants. Will's belly churned when he remembered the burial. Among the family's belongings was a letter from California describing cool green mountains and fertile valleys, addressed to Hiram Beckwith in Missouri. Will and his men left the Beckwiths' graves unmarked for want of usable lumber. Two piles of earth lay beside the Laredo road as the unrecorded end to Hiram Beckwith's dream.

"A damn shame," Carl muttered, riding past the fresh graves. "Killing two old men and a boy. Sumbitches who done it got a taste of ol' Betsy under my coat. Wish we coulda caught up to Zambrano so Betsy had the chance to open his belly, too."

Will shivered in spite of the heat. Carl's shotgun had made a mess of the two men he shot in the river. In many ways Carl was like Leon—he took pleasure in the killing, boasted of it. Were he and Leon the kind of men it took to tame this hostile country? They killed men with the same careless indifference of a traveler who shoots a snake coiled in his path. "Maybe I'm gettin' old," Will sighed under his breath. "I killed my share of Comanches, when I was younger."

Squares of lantern light spilled from the windows of Encinal as they rode to the outskirts. Will signaled a halt and looked for anything amiss. "No wagon," he said, "and no horses in front of the cantina. Looks quiet enough. Let's ride in."

Their horses plodded past the first small adobe, and Will became aware of the silence. No soft music came from the open windows of the cantina. Two burros and a slender mustang pony stood at the hitchrails, swishing flies.

"Mighty quiet," Billy remarked, his palm resting on the butt of his pistol, echoing Will's concern. "It don't seem natural."

Will reined down on the dun and sat, listening to the quiet. A dog barked, announcing their arrival.

"I could use a drink, Cap'n," Carl said, swallowing. "You boys wait here and I'll have a look inside the cantina."

"It's too damn quiet, Carl," Billy warned. Instincts from years as a bounty hunter alerted him.

Will knew he would be a fool to ignore Billy's concerns. "Let's ride around back and take a look," he said, reining his dun off the road.

They rode through the mesquites in single file, keeping to the darkest places, with the lights from the cantina always in sight as they rounded the building. The barking dog followed them from a distance, marking their passage for a careful listener.

Will halted the dun to scan the darkness. The back of the cantina gave off light from the kitchen, where a shattered rear door hung crookedly from rawhide hinges. "Looks okay," Will said. "Nothing wrong with bein' careful. Let's tie these horses and take a look inside."

The men dismounted silently; there was only the occasional rattle of curb chains and the clank of spurs.

"Somebody oughta kill that damn dog," Leon whispered.

Will opened his duster and started forward, alert for the first sign of trouble. Something was bothering him and he couldn't quite put a finger on it now. Perhaps it was only the silence.

Will paused near the back door and waited. No sound came from inside. He peered around the door frame and found the tiny kitchen empty, lighted by a single lantern hung from a beam above a washbasin.

With his hand resting on his gun, he stepped inside on the balls of his feet, to keep his spurs from rattling. Then he crossed the short distance to the doorway into the cantina, and there he hesitated, listening again.

When he rounded the door frame, his eyes flickered around the room. The tables were empty, but as his shadow fell across the floor in the square of light from the kitchen, Will saw a movement near the bar and he whirled toward it, fingers closing around the butt of his Walker.

A dust-laden cowboy stood with his elbows on the bar, a shot glass uplifted. The cowboy sensed Will's presence and turned, the drink poised near his mouth. Will noticed the low-slung gun belt at once, and the slight movement of the cowboy's right hand as it moved closer to ivory hand grips.

"Don't try it," Will warned, a hoarse whisper.

The cowboy's eyes fell to Will's gun hand. "Just having a peaceful drink," the man replied, fingers curled. "No need to go clawing for that gun."

"Maybe," Will said evenly. "Give me some answers first. What's your business in Encinal?"

The cowboy's eyes slitted. "Kind of a nosy bastard, ain't you?"

Will nodded, tensed for trouble. "I get paid to be nosy, stranger. I'm a Texas Ranger. Tell me what you're doing here and I'll see if I've got more questions. There's been some trouble here, and folks don't take kindly to strangers."

Will glanced to a bartender behind the rough-cut plank counter. The old man stood motionless, eyes fixed on him.

"Just passing through," the cowboy remarked. "It's dry around here and I was thirsty."

Again Will took his eyes off the cowboy to examine the bartender's face. "Any trouble?" Will asked.

The old man hesitated too long before he answered. Will knew something was wrong. "Come on in, boys," Will said over his shoulder without looking away from the bar. "Take a good look around. Something don't add up around here."

The cowboy swallowed when Carl and Billy shouldered through the door from the kitchen, spurs clanking on the floor. Will judged the cowboy had almost risked a pull against him with the ivory-handled gun, but when he saw Billy and Carl his face changed.

"What's wrong, Cap'n?" Carl asked, eyeing the stranger as he made his way toward the bar. "This feller givin' you any argument?"

Before Will could answer, Carl's duster flew open and in one swift motion, he brought the sawed-off shotgun up, placing the barrels under the cowboy's chin.

"Take it easy, Carl," Will protested. Too late, Carl cocked the hammers with his thumb.

"He don't look too awful troublesome to me." Carl grinned. The cowboy's eyes walled white as he looked down at the gun.

"I said take it easy," Will snapped. "Take a look around outside, and stay watchful. Where's Leon?"

"Out back," Billy answered. "He ain't got a badge, if you'll remember."

Carl lowered the Greener, and Will looked across the bar. "Is anything wrong?" he asked again.

The bartender pointed to the stranger. "This man asks about Emelio Zambrano. I tell him I don't know nothing," the old man whispered, raising both palms. "He say he kill me if I don't tell him truth."

Carl had started away from the bar, but when he heard the old man's last words, he whirled around and his face turned ugly. "You threatened this old man?" Carl asked angrily. The Greener appeared again suddenly beneath the stranger's jaw. "I oughta blow your damn brains all over this roof," Carl snapped, "threatening an old feller like him."

"Hold it, Carl," Will barked. "Let's find out why this gent is looking for Zambrano."

A silence followed. The cowboy looked from Will's face to Carl's gun. "I heard the name, is all," he answered softly.

Cords stood out on Carl's neck as he pressed the shotgun into the soft flesh below the cowboy's chin. "The cap'n asked you a question, mister," Carl hissed, "and I'm gonna feed your brains to the sparrows if you don't give him an answer that makes sense."

Will was sure he knew the answer before it came. The cowboy was one of the hired guns escorting the wagonload of rifles to Encinal. "I've got a business proposition for Zambrano," the man replied. "A little business down in Mexico."

"Maybe a load of Winchester rifles?" Will asked.

The cowboy tried to shake his head against the pressure of Carl's shotgun. "I don't know nothing about a load of rifles," he protested. "Word is, they're hiring mercenaries down below the border. Zambrano is the name I was given. He's supposed to be here . . . in Encinal."

Will digested the cowboy's story and didn't like the ring of it. "Is that your horse out front at the rail?"

The cowboy nodded.

Will started for the front door. "Keep an eye on him," he said over his shoulder, pausing near the entrance before stepping out into the dark.

The little chestnut mustang stood hipshot, layered with trail dust. Will walked over to examine the cowboy's gear. There was no bedroll behind the saddle, and no canteen. "He didn't come this far without sleeping gear," Will whispered, talking to himself. "If I'm any great shakes as a guesser, that wagon ain't far from town. They sent this feller in to get the lay . . . maybe find Zambrano and bring him out to where they had hidden the wagon."

Will turned on his heel and went back inside. Carl still held the gun to the cowboy's chin, and it was plain the arrangement was making the cowboy uncomfortable.

"Let him go," Will ordered.

Carl blinked. "Did I hear you right, Cap'n?"

"I said let him go. Appears we've got the wrong man. This gent rode in alone."

"But he was askin' for that muderin' Meskin," Carl said. "How else would he know about Zambrano, unless he—"

A look from Will silenced Carl.

Carl lowered his shotgun and gave Will a nod. "Whatever you say, Cap'n," he muttered.

The stranger glared at Carl, then at the others. "This ain't much of a friendly town," he said, trying to sound indignant about it. "I'll be moving on. I can make Laredo by sunup."

He turned back to the bar and tossed down his drink. Glancing once at Will, he made for the door and stalked out.

Will raised a palm to silence the question on Carl's face. They heard the creak of saddle leather as the cowboy mounted, then the sound of horseshoes on hardpan, moving south.

"You know damn well he was one of 'em," Billy remarked, his face to a front window, listening to the hoofbeats fade.

"No gear behind his cantle," Will replied. "He didn't come to this dry country without a canteen and a bedroll. I figure he'll lead us straight to that wagonload of Winchesters. You're the best tracker amongst us, Billy. Give him some lead time, then follow him. If you ain't back at daybreak, we'll pick up your trail. I don't figure the wagon's far from town."

Billy started for the back. "How 'bout if Leon rides along to keep company? Two sets of eyes are better'n one."

Will nodded. "Suits me. Just make sure he keeps his gun holstered. And ride careful. The gent you're following will warn the others that we know about the guns. I tipped my hand when I asked him about rifles. If they strike out for the border, they'll be easy to follow. That wagon is gonna be heavy."

Carl wasted no time ordering a drink. "Give me a bottle of your best, bartender." He tossed a silver dollar on the bar.

Will heard Billy and Leon ride away from the cantina. "I'll see to our horses," he said.

Will led the dun and the roan to an empty corral beside the livery, wondering about the wagon and the guns, trying to guess its whereabouts. "North, I reckon," he mumbled, stripping the saddles from the horses. The stable was dark, and Will entered the barn to fork hay for their mounts as the geldings buried their muzzles in a water trough. The liveryman had gone home for the night. Will could pay the horses' keep in the morning.

He wondered about Isabella as he headed back to the cantina. No lights beckoned behind the windows of the drygoods store, and it was a safe bet that the woman was at home with her father. Will tried to judge which of the adobes might belong to Ben Flowers among the dwellings in Encinal. It would keep till morning, he decided, entering the lamplit cantina.

Carl had engaged the bartender in conversation. "Arturo tells me folks around here are mighty grateful that we came along when we did the other day," Carl announced, a bottle in his fist.

The old man bowed slightly when Will approached the bar. "And tonight, señor," Arturo added. "The hombre said he would kill me unless I told him *la verdad*."

"You folks have had your share of tough customers," Will agreed, taking a shot glass Carl offered, brimming with tequila.

Carl grunted. "Billy and Leon better keep their eyes peeled," he remarked, tossing back a shot. "That owlhoot is a paid gun, or my name ain't Tumlinson. He fancies himself a shootist. There's liable to be more like him around that wagon."

"Billy can take care of himself. A bounty hunter don't live long if he's careless."

Carl frowned. "How come Billy joined the Rangers?"

"He claimed the bounty hunting profession was gettin' crowded. Said he'd had enough of it. After the war it was hard to find an honest job. Hard times made lots of men take chances."

"Yeah . . . the damn war ended a bunch of things," Carl agreed softly, thoughtfully. "I came back to a burned-out farm and my little brother's grave. I had to make a living somehow, so I signed on with a cow outfit headed north. I've seen a lot of country, but wasn't none of it mine. Never will be, I don't reckon. Not at twenty dollars a month. How 'bout you, Cap'n? How come you're a Ranger?"

Will shrugged. "Same reason as you, I reckon. No place to settle after the war . . . my folks lost their farm to carpetbaggers before I could get home from Tennessee. Wasn't much of a farm anyways, so I don't reckon it matters. My paw followed a team of mules all his life. After the war, the idea didn't suit me. The Confederate Army taught me one thing—how to use a gun. I hired out to the Rangers to fight Comanches. It was something I knew how to do, and it was the only job I could find at the time."

Carl shook his head like he understood. "Not many men can stomach this sort of life, Cap'n. It takes a special breed. I figure the four of us are cut from the same rough cloth."

"There's just three of us now," Will replied. "Leon's finished as a Ranger, and I'll do the same to any man who can't follow orders. Leon didn't leave me choices . . . I had to take his badge."

"I sorta figured you'd change your mind, Cap'n. I had it figured you would."

Will shook his head. "Leon swore an oath to uphold the law when that badge was pinned on his chest. His memory got too short and it cost him the job."

Carl poured another round of drinks. "Him an' Billy been friends for years. Billy's liable to turn in his badge when we get back to San Antone."

Will didn't answer, or try to guess the outcome. Leaning elbows on the bar, he sipped tequila and wondered about the wagon.

Later, as he and Carl sat at a corner table, he thought about Isabella again, to pass the time. When the business with the guns was finished, he meant to take another bath and pay the lovely Isabella Flowers a social call.

Chapter Nine

A pungent odor awakened Will. He had nodded off to sleep in his chair. He found the source of the smell when his eyes focused. Carl was dressing his thigh wound with salve from a tiny jar.

"Doc Warren sold me this stuff," Carl said, grimacing. "It stinks worse'n a skunk, but the doc claimed it'll keep my leg from swelling."

Will glanced toward a window. The sky was dark. "How long did I sleep?" he asked, stretching to rid his body of stiffness.

"Couple of hours. Ol' Arturo went home . . . gave us the run of the place, seein' as we were the only customers. Said if he couldn't trust a couple of Rangers, he couldn't trust nobody."

Will stood up slowly, rewarded by pain in his knees and ankles. "Any sign of Billy and Leon?"

Carl shook his head.

"I figured they'd be back by now . . . didn't figure that wagon would be far."

"They'll be along," Carl replied, closing the salve jar.

"My belly's empty," Will groused, rubbing his stomach. "I'll see what I can rustle up in the kitchen."

Will hobbled past the bar on sleep-deadened legs, wincing when the pain in his joints argued against travel. Entering the kitchen, he found a sulfur match and lit the lantern. A rack of drying *cabrito* hung above the woodstove, prepared with a coating of chilies and salt. Will took strips of goatmeat back to their table in a tin plate.

They ate in silence, washing the meat down with tequila. Will worried about Billy and Leon, finally dozing again until dawn awakened him.

"I figure we better get mounted," Will said, tossing coins on the bar to pay for the food and drink. "Something's keeping Billy and Leon too long."

Will limped out the door to saddle the horses. Carl limped beside him, and Will thought them an unsightly pair, two cripples in dust-coated attire, unwashed, saddle sore. As they made their way across the road, Will was distracted by someone's approach. His eyes came to rest on a woman walking from one of the adobes and he recognized her at once, long brown hair flowing in an early breeze.

"Why, good morning, Captain Dobbs," Isabella said, her face breaking into a smile.

Will halted and tucked his duster about him, wishing he were most anyplace else just then, rumpled and dirty like he was.

"Good morning, ma'am," he replied, suddenly aware of the new stubble on his chin. He took a step sideways to be downwind.

"Have you come back to look into the story the boy told about the rifles?" she asked.

"That's where we're headed now, Miss Flowers. Last night we met up with a gent who figures to be one of the men with the wagon. Two of my men followed him away from Encinal. We hoped he'd lead us to the guns."

A gust of wind drew Isabella's white blouse against the swell of her breasts. Will caught himself looking down . . . and quickly righted his glance, to seem proper. It was not possible that the woman was even prettier than he remembered, and yet as he looked into her eyes, he felt his knees turn to jelly. Isabella's skin was without a flaw, like creamed coffee in a china cup. Will swallowed when his throat ran dry.

"The people of Encinal owe you and your men a great debt," she said, and now her smile was gone and her face serious. "We can offer only our hospitality, and our gratitude. It was a sad day for Encinal when we buried three of its people. Yet each of us knows there could have been so many more, had you not arrived. You have our thanks, Captain."

Carl limped to the corral and caught the horses, bridling Will's dun for the saddling. "I'd better get going, ma'am," Will mumbled, the words getting tangled on his tongue. He tipped his hat brim and tried to walk away like a much younger man, without the stiffness of old age hampering his strides.

"Please come to my father's store when your business is over, Captain Dobbs," she said to his back. "Perhaps you will join us for supper?"

"I'd like that," he replied, entering the corral.

Isabella hurried off with the wind in her skirt, outlining her slender legs with the fabric. Will stared at her until she rounded a corner behind the blacksmith's shop. When Will turned to saddle the dun, he found Carl grinning.

"Your eyes damn near popped right out of your head, Cap'n." Carl chuckled. "I'm of the opinion that the woman has taken a fancy to you."

Will ignored the remark, embarrassed by it. He swung his saddle over the dun's back and busied himself with the cinch.

They were mounted and moving south along fresh sets of hoofprints when Will sighted the dust sign to the west. "Somebody's comin'," he said, pointing.

Two riders galloped through the brush, topping a rolling hill west of town. "Billy and Leon," Carl announced. Will had already made the identification.

The pair rode up to Will and Carl, sliding their winded mounts to a halt. "We found the wagon, Captain," Billy said. "It's a couple of hours west, in an arroyo. Worst is, they've got maybe a dozen outriders. They started breaking camp soon as the cowboy we jumped hit the arroyo. They know we're onto them, and they're clearin' out quick as they can."

"Which way?" Will asked, knowing the answer.

"South," Billy replied, "toward the border."

Will grimaced. A dozen paid guns would be a handful.

"There's four of us," Carl remarked. "Those ain't the best odds, but we can handle it."

"Only three," Will replied. "Leon's out of it now."

Billy's face darkened. "How come you're bein' so all-fired mule-headed, Will? Just hand Leon his badge and there'll be four of us again."

Will shot Billy a warning look. "The badge stays in my shirt, Billy, and that's the end of it. Let's ride!"

Will spurred off and Carl swung in behind. Billy and Leon exchanged words, then they hit a lope to join the others, riding through the dust from the leaders' horses.

They saw the dust sign from the wagon and reined south to head it off, spurring lathered horses, riding hard. Will knew it was senseless to form a plan until he saw the lay of things and the outriders. A running gun battle against a dozen men would be too risky. He'd have to figure another way to stop the wagon without putting his men in a war they stood slim chances of winning. He hadn't counted on so many men guarding the rifles. It was proof that the guns were bringing high prices as contraband.

Leading his men south, Will knew their horses were sending a telltale warning into the morning sky. Like the wagon, progress was marked by boiling caliche. The wagon guards would be ready. It promised to be an all-out fight, three Rangers against twelve paid gunmen, over who would lay claim to the guns.

On a rise above the chalky desert flats to the west they saw the wagon moving forward at a trot, pulled by a four-horse team. Will sighted the fanned outriders, circling the wagon. Rifles glinted in the sunlight—the guards were alerted, guns drawn and ready.

Will drew rein to let the horses blow. Dust caked to the animals' sweat-soaked hides. Carl's roan coughed, gasping for air. A bit clattered in a gelding's muzzle, curb chain rattling.

Will pulled his Winchester, a .44, chambered for the same

loads as his Walker. He worked the lever and saw the gleam of a brass cartridge.

Leon nudged his horse alongside Will's. "Me an' Billy've been talking," Leon began. "I don't figure you'll stop me if I lend a hand just now. I know I ain't a Ranger anymore, but I can still use a gun. Just thought I'd mention it."

Will was caught betwixt and between. Another gun could make the difference in the battle about to be waged. "Right now I can't think of much argument against the idea." Will sighed, viewing the irregular line of riders fanning out in front of the wagon. "I won't try to stop you, but it don't change a thing."

Leon shook his head. He pulled his Winchester and worked the mechanism, dropping the hammer gently with his thumb.

"Spread out," Will commanded. "Hold your fire until I give the word. If I get the chance, I aim to talk to whoever's in charge of the wagon—warn 'em to turn back. If they'll allow it, those guns can go back to Kansas without any bloodshed."

Carl grunted. "Ain't likely, Cap'n. They'll figure they've got us outnumbered, so they can shoot their way through."

"Maybe," Will replied, eyeing the wagon. "I'll try to talk to 'em first, but if the shootin' starts, I want you down off those horses so you can steady your aim. We'll take down as many as we can and then pull back. Make every shot count."

Billy and Leon rode off the rise at a trot. Will waited until they reached the flats, then he nodded to Carl and they touched spurs to their horses' flanks. Dust plumed from the heels of the horses as Will and his men formed a ragged line across the wagon's path.

A gust of dry wind carried the sounds of harness chain. Will saw a man at the front of the outriders raise his hand to halt the wagon. Brakes squealed against iron-rimmed wheels as the freighter ground to a stop.

For a time the two groups watched each other, just out of rifle range, two armies ready to engage when a signal was given. Will understood the risks if he rode forward to identify himself as a Texas Ranger, but he meant to give it a try.

"Looks like we've got 'em buffaloed," Carl announced, off to Will's right by twenty yards.

Will didn't answer, as two outriders came together to talk. He counted the men spread across the plain. Thirteen horsemen and a wagon driver with a rifle across his lap. "I'll see if I can get close enough to talk them into turning back," Will shouted. "If a shot gets fired, I want you down off those horses, making sure of your targets."

He urged the dun forward, waving a hand over his head to signal the outriders that he wanted a parley. There was only the slimmest of chances that fourteen paid gunmen could be turned aside by four Rangers, but he was duty-bound to give it a try.

The distance shortened, still just beyond the range of a rifle, when one of the gunmen brought a gun to his shoulder.

"Look out, Will!" Carl cried behind him.

The rifle popped and Will reined down hard on the dun. A puff of gun smoke reeled away on the wind.

A horseman started forward, then more. A whip cracked and the wagon rumbled toward Will. Rifle barrels bristled, drawn quickly from saddle boots. Another gunshot sounded, and Will wheeled the dun to a lope.

He galloped back to join the others and swung around to face the wagon. When he judged the range was right, he gave the order. "Get down!"

Rifles cracked as Will and his men took aim. Will sighted and fired. On either side Carl and Leon triggered shots. Will's target fell.

Angry shouts echoed down the line of riders. Will levered another shell and swung his gunsights. Rifles popped in the distance as Will triggered off a second shot. A galloping paint horse at the front of the charging pack stumbled, tossing the cowboy on its back. Bullets sang overhead as Will chambered again, sweeping his gun barrel, searching for the target.

"Got the sumbitch!" Carl cried above the din. An empty

shell casing flew from Will's rifle soundlessly. He sought a rider in the swirling dust, waiting.

Leon's rifle barked to Will's left and a rider went down. A running horse buckled at the front of the charge, going to its knees suddenly, sending its rider skyward as if he'd sprouted wings.

"Fall back!" Will shouted, whirling toward the snorting dun, trying to mount the skittish animal as guns thundered and bullets whined overhead. Will stuck a boot in a stirrup and swung aboard. A chunk of speeding lead whistled close. The skirmish had served its purpose—by Will's count, seven riders were out of the fight. "Fall back!" he cried again, reining the frightened dun for a last hasty shot into the oncoming charge.

Carl struggled aboard his roan, slowed down by the bad leg. Billy was already in his saddle. Leon stood calmly and sent a shot toward the line of riders. "Get mounted!" Will barked. A rider toppled slowly into the dust behind his galloping sorrel. Will heard a cry of pain as the cowboy disappeared.

Leon swung to the bay's back and drove spurs into its ribs. Lunging, the bay broke into an all-out run. Will held his dun until Carl spurred past him in a cloud of dust. The dun needed no urging to reach full stride behind Carl's roan.

Open flats lay in front of them—no cover in sight where Will and his men could make a stand. East, a bald knob jutted from the prairie. Will reined the dun and rode for the hill, swinging a look over his shoulder.

Riderless horses galloped aimlessly in all directions, trailing reins. Will searched the boiling dust for signs of pursuit and found nothing. He slowed the dun and squinted. Five mounted men brought their horses to a halt on the plain behind Will. A lame cowboy hobbled back toward the wagon without his horse. The charge had been broken by well-placed shots, a Comanche tactic that all too often humbled a superior force of cavalry—attack and fall back, making every shot count. Will Dobbs and Travis Hollaman learned the lesson early, when they first fought the Kwahadies for the Llano River country around Fort Mason.

Will slowed the dun and reined to a halt at the base of the knob. A crippled horse limped away from the battle scene, favoring a foreleg. The five riders sat their winded mounts a quarter mile from the wagon, talking things over, gesturing with rifles.

Will heard Carl gallop up behind him. "We routed 'em, Cap'n," Carl shouted. "There ain't no fight left in them. Let's ride back and take them rifles."

"Won't be quite that easy," Will remarked. A wounded man tried to stand beside the carcass of a horse. Another sat up holding his shoulder.

Billy and Leon galloped to the knob. Billy's bay coughed. A trickle of blood ran down the bay's rump from a slice across the animal's croup. "My horse got nicked," Billy explained. "He's travelin' kinda ouchy, but he'll heal. I'd say we got off lucky."

"I don't figure it's over yet," Will warned, sighting the five wagon guards as they split to ride through the wounded scattered over the battlefield. "Reload, men. Those guns are stayin' right here until they surrender that wagon."

For a time the men were silent, thumbing cartridges into the loading gates of Winchesters. Sweating horses lowered their heads to gulp air. Will kept an eye on the riders. Two wounded men were helped up behind saddles. One rider skirted west to gather loose horses, but the wagon was stopped. The driver made no move to advance southward.

"They'll be a little smarter this time," Billy observed. "I don't figure they'll charge us again."

Will nodded. "We'll have to nip their flanks. We've got the advantage now. They've got a mighty heavy wagon to move, and the odds are just about even. There's a lot of open country to cross to reach the border. Those men and horses will need water. I'd say we're holding all the aces."

Morning heat had begun to build, increasing the feeding frenzy of the *chichadas*. Heat waves began to dance from the pale caliche. Will listened to the screams of the locusts. A hot wind fluttered the trails of his duster about his legs, tossing the manes and tails of the horses.

"Those men don't know dry country," Leon explained. "That gent we jumped at the cantina last night is from up north someplace. Ain't none of 'em carryin' canteens on their saddles. It won't take long for 'em to get mighty thirsty."

"They've got water kegs hangin' off the wagon," Carl said, pointing. "A shooter could fill 'em full of holes if he got close enough, but I'm of the opinion that we took the fight out of 'em just now. Yankee cowboys ain't got much backbone, in my experience. Won't surprise me none if they turn tail and run."

Will watched the men return to the wagon. Wounded were helped to the ground, seated in the shade from the wagonbed. "They'll talk things over," Will said. "If that wagon moves, we'll give them another taste of lead."

Leon scowled. "There's another way, Cap'n. One man with a rifle could belly closer through those cactus patches and start dropping them harness horses when he got in range. They can't move the wagon if the harness is full of dead horses."

Will shook his head quickly. "I never was much for killing horses. We'll find a better way to get the job done. The odds are with us now. We'll wait them out. The next move is theirs."

The men around the wagon milled about, faces turned toward the knob where Will and his men waited. It promised to be a long day, if Will was any judge of things. A waiting game, to see who made the next fatal mistake.

Chapter Ten

Without shade the heat was merciless, unyielding, moving in hot blasts on a southwesterly wind. Horses suffered, as did the men wrapped in canvas dusters. Tails to the wind, the horses held muzzles to the ground, seeking their own meager shade. By mid-afternoon Will's lips were cracked. When he ran his tongue over them, he heard a dry, brittle sound.

"I'd give a month's pay for a bottle of whiskey," Carl groaned, turning in his saddle, looking in the direction of Encinal with a wistful gaze.

Billy took a single mouthful of water from his canteen. A horse stamped its hoof impatiently. The sounds of the *chichadas* ebbed and flowed on gusts of wind, feeding on scrub mesquite brush, clinging to windblown limbs.

"Those goddamn bugs are gonna drive me crazy," Carl said, casting an evil look around.

In the distance they could see riderless horses tied to the wheels of the wagon. Men were huddled in the wagon's shade like ants, hats pulled low to shield their eyes from the blowing dust. The standoff dragged on into the afternoon hours. Buzzards circled and then swept down to feed on the carcasses of dead horses and men on the plain. Will watched a big black bird perch atop a dead horse to peck out its eye. His gaze shifted aimlessly, halting briefly where buzzards fed on the body of a man sprawled on a patch of barren caliche. The carcass moved eerily when the birds ripped flesh from the chest cavity—arms jerked with false life. Booted feet twitched.

"Hell of a sight, ain't it?" Billy asked quietly. "Reminds me of Second Bull Run. Vultures turned the sky black as night. Some of the younger boys tried to shoot them when they landed on a dead Reb. It was okay for 'em to eat Yanks, but not the boys in gray."

"Hard thing to watch," Will sighed, turning away. "Don't take long to get a bellyful."

"Somebody's movin'," Leon remarked.

Two men swung up and reined horses away from the wagon. The pair rode north, keeping their horses in a shuffling trot. Wind made curls of the dust from the horses' heels.

"Deserters," Will guessed. "A paid gun ain't got any loyalty. Those two figured the pay wasn't high enough to be worth dying for."

"We can take that damn wagon now, Cap'n," Carl said. "I count six men under that wagon, and two of 'em are wounded."

Will cast a look toward the sun. "Let the heat do the job for us," he replied. "No sense risking a bullet if there's another way."

"My throat's gettin' mighty dry," Carl argued. "I'd sooner risk a bullet as die of thirst."

Will didn't answer. Resting his palms on his saddle horn, he watched the wagon. Patience was a lesson to be learned when the enemy was in a stronger position. Time weighed heavily on the shoulders of foolish men, and they made hasty mistakes. The war had taught him patience, and then came the unforgettable lessons learned fighting Comanches. Patient men lived to fight another day.

His dun coughed, awakening him from a hazy daydream. Will blinked and focused on the wagon. Men were moving, and the sight brought him fully alert. "They're mounting up," Will warned.

Five riders swung a leg over saddles. A sixth man lay flat beneath the wagon. Will stiffened and pulled his Winchester from the saddle boot. Carl and Billy drew their rifles.

One rider swung away from the wagon and rode toward the Rangers at a trot. The others sat their mounts near the wagonbed, looking toward the knob. Then the lone horseman spurred his mount to an easy lope. "They've decided to talk to us," Will observed, "maybe try to strike a deal."

The rider galloped closer, and now Will could see his face. A red beard was chalked by caliche. His hat covered his eyes with shadow until he drew rein a dozen yards from Will.

For a moment the rider sat to survey the group before him. He looked from Will to the others, then back again. "You boys done some mighty good shootin'," he said. "My men ain't exactly city slickers with guns, but you whupped us good an' proper. You can have the wagon and the rifles. All I'm askin' is to ride away without more trouble. I've got a couple of men hurt bad. If I don't get them to a doctor right soon, they'll bleed to death. I'll have a bunch of explainin' to do about the guns, but I'd rather do some tall talking than die for 'em. This country is the hottest son of a bitch I ever saw."

"Who sent the Winchesters?" Will asked.

The cowboy shook his head. "That ain't part of the trade. I said you could have the guns, but I ain't gonna sing like I was leadin' a church choir out here."

"A name," Will growled. "You can give me the name and ride off, or I'll place you under arrest."

The cowboy's face hardened. "Stiles said you were Rangers. I still say I'm offering a fair swap—those guns for my men's lives. Think it over."

"I already did," Will answered. "It's my job to stop guns headed for the revolution down in Mexico. We know the rifles came from Stanford Arms in Kansas City. Now tell me who paid you to bring them to the border."

The cowboy looked around him, then over his shoulder to the wagon. Finally he faced Will and his shoulders sagged.

"A feller by the name of Hickok hired us," he began. "We met at Dodge City a few months back, and he set the deal up for us to ride shotgun on this load of rifles. He wired Stanford a month ago and said he was sheriff of Laredo now, and to bring the wagon to a place called Encinal, where we'd meet up with a Mexican by the name of Zambrano. It was supposed to be Zambrano's job to take the rifles across the border, only we hit bad weather and had to wait for some swollen streams to go down. Stiles said this Zambrano wasn't in Encinal, but the place was crawlin' with Texas Rangers."

Will nodded. "Your story fits."

"Hickok was supposed to give us the rest of our money when we got the guns safe to Encinal."

"Hickok's gone," Will replied. "He ran into a little trouble with us and he lit out for parts unknown. I don't figure you'll get the rest of your pay."

The cowboy shook his head. "It appears you Rangers deal out more'n your share of misery in these parts. I never figured there was anybody who could shoot like you boys done. You've got my word on one thing, Ranger—I won't be back to this godforsaken place again. I've seen all of Texas I ever care to see."

Will lifted his gaze to the wagon. "Load your wounded and clear out. The closest doctor is south, at Laredo. A day's ride. Ask for Doc Warren. If you come back this way again with more guns headed to Mexico, I'll see to it that you do some time for it. Remember what I said."

The red-bearded cowboy shook his head, sleeving sweat from his brow. "If that's the only worry you've got, then you ain't got any, Ranger. I ain't comin' back. There's easier pickings elsewhere."

A buzzard flapped clumsily from one carcass to another, and it was a reminder of unfinished business. "What about your dead?"

The cowboy cast a look over his shoulder. "A man'd have to be crazy to try an' dig a grave in this heat. Leave 'em for the buzzards. I've got wounded to attend to."

Will watched the cowboy gather his reins and wheel his mustang toward the wagon. Hooves rattled across dry ground as the man loped his horse away from the knob.

"Let's ride in," Will said. "Keep your guns handy, just in case those gents have a change of heart."

Will and his men rode off the knob into a blast of wind. At the wagon a prone cowboy was hoisted over an empty saddle belly down, arms dangling lifelessly. "That feller won't survive the ride to Laredo," Carl observed. Another rider was slumped over his horse's withers, obviously pained.

Will's dun snorted as it neared the carcass of a horse where vultures fed. A bird squawked, hopping from the path of the oncoming horses. Will wrinkled his nose, for the heat had already begun to bloat the corpses. Blowflies lifted, then fell back in black swarms.

The wagon guards gave the Rangers a wide berth as they rode south away from the wagon. Will recognized the one called Stiles hunkered down to ride into the wind. Will halted the dun in front of the wagon teams to watch the gunmen depart. Down deep he knew there was no fight left in them, but it paid to be careful.

"Bucket some water from those kegs for the harness horses," Will ordered. "If there's enough to go around, we'll water our mounts before we start for Encinal. Carl, I want you driving the wagon."

Will rode to the back of the freighter and swung down. A tarp was tied over the wagonbed. When one corner was freed, Will glimpsed freshly-milled wooden crates. The smell of oil wafted from the wagonbed, and the faint odor of pine. It was an odd time to remember the name on the manifest, yet it came to him then. A man by the name of Porfirio Ortega had paid for four hundred rifles that he would never see. Ortega's support for the revolution had come to nothing, ending forty miles from the Mexican border. The guns had certainly cost Ortega a fortune when Hickok added his price for safe passage.

Leon and Billy bucketed water for the four harness horses. Carl climbed stiffly to the wagon seat, wincing when he put weight on his bad leg.

"Both water kegs were damn near dry," Leon remarked. "Those fellers weren't none too smart about dry country, Cap'n."

They gave mouthfuls of water to their mounts and readied for the drive to Encinal. Carl slapped reins over the rumps of the team, and the wagon creaked and rattled off, wheels cutting deep ruts in the caliche. Will rode to the front and swung east with the sun at his back. Once, starting over a rise, he looked south, where the wagon guards were mere specks on the horizon.

They entered Encinal before dusk on trail-weary horses. The teams labored to pull the heavy freighter the last mile, lathered, leaning into their harness under the crack of Carl's whip. Will led the procession to the front of the cantina, where he raised a hand and swung down.

Curious people stopped along the street to stare at the wagon and the dust-laden men. Will crossed to the livery. A withered Mexican greeted him with a slight bow.

"See to the care of our horses," Will said, digging in his pocket for coins.

"Si, señor," the old man replied, taking the money in a gnarled hand.

Will turned and came face to face with Isabella Flowers. The sight of her caught him by surprise, flustered him. Dried sweat made mud of the caliche on his face and neck. He self-consciously tried to brush it off with the back of his hand. "I'm a mess," he stammered, unaccountably edgy. Isabella smiled, and Will's plight only worsened. Her beautiful face crinkled, and his knees went weak.

"You found the guns?" she asked.

Will nodded. His feet fidgeted, beyond his control until he heard his spurs rattle. He forced his boots still.

Isabella's face darkened. "My father says Zambrano will come back for his rifles. He worries that there will be more trouble in Encinal."

"Isn't likely," Will replied, distracted by Carl's limping strides toward the cantina. "We'll take the guns back to San Antone when we leave. I need to send a wire to Captain Hollaman in Laredo to tell him we have the wagon. Who runs the little telegraph office down the street?"

Isabella chuckled. "Our priest. Father Tomas knew the language of the telegraph key before the Church sent him here. No one else understands the talking wire. Father Tomas will open the office for you. Encinal is a small village, Captain Dobbs. The telegraph is hardly ever used."

"I reckon I oughta get myself a bath first, before I see the priest. I've got one clean shirt left in my saddlebags. Maybe later, after I get myself cleaned up, you could show me where Father Tomas lives?"

She tilted her head, a hint of laughter in her eyes. "Yes, Captain. After you've had a bath."

She was gone before he could think of more to say. He watched her hips sway as she walked toward her father's store. Her hair bounced on her shoulders.

"Buy you a drink, Cap'n," Billy said, leaning against a hitchrail, a look of amusement on his face. "You look like you could use one. Maybe it's the sun, but it appears your face got red just now. Hard to tell under all that mud."

Will trudged across the road, face lowered, wondering if he had indeed turned red in Isabella's presence. The woman had an unnerving effect on him, and he discovered one of the few instances in his memory when he was not in complete control of things.

"Let's open a jug," Will muttered, passing Billy at the rail. "Wash some of this dust from our throats."

They entered the cool darkness of the adobe and found Carl at the bar, resting his elbows. A bottle was already three inches from the top in front of him. Leon sat off to himself at a corner table nursing a jug of mescal. Seeing Leon alone reminded Will of the part he played in today's brush with death fighting the wagon guards. He'd thrown in with them no differently than when he wore a badge.

Will took the bottle in front of Carl and inclined his head toward Leon's table. "Let's drink one together . . . the four of us."

Leon watched Will and the others approach the table, and just then Will wished for a way to reinstate the maverick Ranger without violating the mandates of his conscience. "You did a hell of a job out there today, Leon," Will said, drawing back an empty chair. Billy placed empty shot glasses on the tabletop. "I owe you. I wish there was some way to pin this badge back on your chest."

Leon toyed with his glass. "I done what I figured was right when it come to that little girl, Cap'n. It stuck in my craw that she was with Zambrano. Wasn't right to leave her there."

Will closed his eyes and bit down. To a simple cowboy like Leon the river was just water and his choice had seemed easy enough. Major Peoples would never understand why Leon's brain couldn't grasp the idea of an invisible boundary he couldn't cross to mete out justice. "It wasn't right to leave her with Zambrano, but it was the law."

"Law oughta be changed then," Leon replied. "A dogshit Mexican steals a little girl in Texas, there oughta be a way to get her back inside the law, seems like."

Billy poured drinks without offering comment, but Carl's face turned ugly. "Leon did what he figured was right, Will," Carl said hotly. "He's got more backbone than any of us. You're takin' a hard line on it, Cap'n."

"Got no choice," Will said softly, wishing otherwise.

"Here's to luck," Billy toasted, lifting his glass.

"Luck," Will sighed. "And here's to Leon for throwing in with us today."

They tossed back shots and rested their glasses. When Leon looked across the table at Will, Will squirmed. Leon was crazy, but his courage went beyond the touch of madness that made him enjoy killing. He'd known the dangers of stalking Zambrano on his home range.

Arturo hurried toward them with a platter of warm tortillas and a bowl of picante. The food took everyone's thoughts from the discussion of Leon's badge, and Will was as grateful as he was hungry. They dove into the tortillas and hot sauce ravenously while Arturo lit a lantern. The cerrano peppers did their work, and in short order eyes watered around the table as men sought to put out the fires with swallows of tequila and mescal.

"What'll we do with the guns?" Carl asked around a mouthful of tortilla.

"Drive them back to San Antone. I'll wire Captain Hollaman that we've got them, and advise him of what we learned about Hickok, in case Hickok shows up around Laredo again. There's a priest who runs the telegraph. Isabella is gonna take me to him after I wash the dust off my hide."

Carl grinned. "You ain't very pretty just now, Cap'n, if you'll excuse me for gettin' it said. If I was goin' courtin' a pretty young gal, I'd damn sure take a bath and shave off my chin whiskers afore I done it."

"There isn't any courting going on," Will protested feebly. "She hasn't shown the slightest bit of interest in an old man like me."

Carl shook his head, grinning possumlike. "That ain't the way it looks to the rest of us. That gal has taken a fancy to you, Cap'n. I can see it on her face. Hell, a blind man can see she has taken a hankerin' to you. It's as plain as a wart on a pig's snout."

Will felt his face turn hot. "You're wrong," he said, hoping otherwise.

Chapter Eleven

He soaked himself in a stone and mortar water trough behind the livery. A two-sided shelter offered privacy. He shaved by lantern light, peering at his reflection in a shard of mirror on the back wall of the stable. He donned his remaining clean shirt, a gray bib front missing two buttons, then he shook the dust out of his denims and pulled them on. He combed through his tangled mane and did the best job he could with it in bad light. Streaks of gray ran through his black curls, offending in the image he saw in the mirror, a reminder of advancing age. "Gettin' old, Dobbs," he muttered to himself as he buckled on his gun.

Dark came as he trudged back to the cantina, and with the dark came a skyful of twinkling stars. Lantern light glowed from half a hundred windows in the village, spilling from uncurtained openings onto the caliche. Goats bleated in the pens east of town, begging for cornstalks and water. Somewhere a dog barked and a kid goat cried for milk. A cool breeze belied the hot winds he and his men suffered earlier in the day, and the locusts were mercifully silent now.

He joined the others in the cantina and poured himself a stiff drink, thus preparing himself for the meeting with lovely Isabella when she showed him to the priest's quarters.

"You look a sight better." Carl grinned. "Maybe the lady won't have to pinch her nose when you go a-courting."

He ignored Carl's needling and downed his drink, deciding upon another for good measure, should Isabella happen to stand too close.

"The cap'n is drinkin' up the nerve to ask her to marry him," Carl continued.

Will shoved back his chair and stood up. "I'm wiring Laredo. Keep an eye on those guns, just in case. The Flowers woman says her father thinks Zambrano will come back for his rifles."

Carl shook his head. "That Meskin's got his tail between his legs after what we gave him. And then ol' Leon went over and let him have another dose of Texas Ranger lead. Zambrano won't tangle with us again, Cap'n. I'd bet a month's pay on it."

Will walked out of the cantina and turned for Ben Flowers's store. Lights still burned behind the windows, and the front door was propped open to admit the cool night breeze. Then he saw a woman sweeping the front porch and recognized her. In spite of the previous drinks, his throat was dry.

"Evening, ma'am," he said, catching her attention, tipping his hat when she turned.

"Good evening, Captain Dobbs. Are you ready to talk to Father Tomas?" she asked, leaning her broom against the wall.

"I need to get off that wire," he replied, hooking his thumbs in his gun belt to keep his hands occupied.

"Come with me," she said, dusting off her hands, straightening the front of her blouse, lifting it higher where it revealed too much of her bosom. She stepped off the porch lightly and made a turn for the east end of town, where the goats bleated. Will walked beside her, scenting a hint of perfume when she pushed a stray lock of hair from her forehead. "Father Tomas lives near our goats, to watch over them at night when the coyotes prowl near the pens. He loves animals, even the lowliest burro. He talks to the chickens when he scatters their grain in the mornings, telling them it is God's will that they must lay many eggs. The children make fun of him, talking to chickens, thinking no one is listening."

Isabella's lilting voice carried musically on the breeze

above the cries of the goats. Will stole glances at her when he guessed she wasn't looking.

They came to a tiny one-room adobe hut. A candle flickered through one window. The sounds of their footsteps brought a shadow to the open doorway.

"Good evening, my child," a gentle voice said. Father Tomas stood, hands folded, until they reached his porch. "I see you have brought one of the Rangers."

"Yes, Father," Isabella replied. "This is Captain Will Dobbs. He asks that you unlock the telegraph office so he may send a message to Laredo."

"Of course," the priest said quickly, stepping from his doorway. Will saw his face clearly in the light from the stars. The priest was old, past sixty, a withered, leathery face darkened by years in the sun. "There is no line to Laredo, my son," he said as they started toward the office. "A line runs to San Antonio. From there, your message can be sent to Laredo."

"Just so it gets there," Will replied. "I need to advise the Ranger post that we have the wagonload of rifles."

"Ah, yes . . . the rifles little Pedro spoke to me about, and just one day before the boy died. I warned Pedro to stay away from the cantina while those bandits were here, but he did not listen. And he paid dearly, with his life."

Will took a deep breath, remembering the boy they found facedown in the street, and his mother's anguished cries. Will sighed. "We did the only thing we could, Father Tomas. We were sorry about the boy."

"I understand, Captain," the priest replied, hobbling over the caliche in worn sandals, his brown monk's cloak dragging softly behind him in the dust. "Some men yield only to the sword, I'm afraid. Many more of these humble people might have died, had you and your men not come. It was unfortunate . . . about little Pedro. Oh, how his mother grieves for him now!"

The priest removed a key from inside his garment and unlocked the door to the office. A sulfur match sputtered when Father Tomas lit a lantern. The adobe was a ten-foot square with a small desk its only furnishing. On the desk was the telegraph key, thick with spiderwebs, and beside it a rusted iron generator attached by dusty wires.

"Write down your message, Captain," Father Tomas said, pulling spiderwebs away carefully with a crook of a finger. He twisted the generator crank several times and tapped tentatively on the key until the sound was just right to his practiced ear. "I was taught the telegraph code, for I was message carrier for the Franciscans before God called me here. San Antonio will answer me if the line is in good repair. Diego and Paulito joined the wire where it was cut by the bandits. Write your message, and I will do the best I can to send it through."

The key tapped an answer and Father Tomas smiled. "All is ready now, my son. Give me your message. The day after tomorrow is Sunday. The only payment I ask of you for the use of the telegraph is that you join us for mass on Sunday morning."

From the corner of his eye Will saw Isabella smile. "Will you stay until Sunday?" she asked.

He shrugged. "Our horses could use a rest, I reckon. I suppose an extra day won't matter."

Father Tomas shook his head. "And you will have a priest's blessing for your journey homeward."

Will gave the brief message to the priest and watched the old man tap the key, aware of Isabella's closeness in the confines of the little room, for she stood at his elbow to watch Father Tomas work the telegraph, and the sweet smell of her perfume drew his attention. The priest was intent upon his task, hunched over the key reading Will's scribbled note, permitting Will to steal glances at the woman unnoticed. The perfection of her face fascinated him, her uplifted nose and flawless skin, full lips slightly parted, a face framed by long brown hair flowing to her creamy shoulders. A cleft between her breasts reflected sparkles of lantern light, dewy with tiny drops of perspiration where her blouse hemmed. The telegraph key clicked, yet Will's thoughts were elsewhere—wondering what Isabella would be like in his arms, gazing up at him with one of her beautiful smiles, then with her arms moving snakelike around his neck as he bent to kiss her.

The clicking of the key ended abruptly, and so did Will's short fantasy. "The message is sent," Father Tomas said. "The operator in San Antonio will confirm that it has been received."

A silent minute passed. Will scowled at the telegraph, for it seemed there would be no confirmation from San Antonio. "Maybe the line is down somewhere?" he suggested.

Before the priest could answer, there was a single click, then two more in rapid succession. "It is done," Father Tomas said. "Now they will send it to Laredo. My work is finished."

"Thanks, Father." Will said, digging in his pocket for a coin. "I'll make a little contribution to the church for the inconvenience. I appreciate your time."

He handed the priest a silver coin and turned for the door.

"May God bless you, my son," Father Tomas replied, tucking the coin into a pocket of his robe. He extinguished the lantern as Will and Isabella walked outside. The padlock sounded behind them.

"We will walk with you, Father," Isabella said. "It is a very beautiful night."

The priest smiled. "It is indeed, and I will enjoy your company."

They started back toward the bleating goats, their backs to the cooling breeze. The priest's sandals crunched softly, making Will conscious of the much louder rattle of his spur rowels, whereas Isabella's feet were soundless. Passing between adobe dwellings, Father Tomas turned unexpectedly. "Forgive the delay, but I must first put out the candles at the shrine of the Virgin."

"Of course, Father," Isabella replied, smiling up at Will in the darkness. "Captain Dobbs won't mind a few extra steps, will you?"

The breeze fluttered her hair about her shoulders, and Will almost forgot to answer her question. "I'm in no hurry," he replied, thinking how he might enjoy walking all the way to

San Antonio if he could share Isabella's company. All sorts of foolish notions had begun to enter his thoughts now, standing close to the woman like he was.

The priest led them past rows of adobe huts, toward a much larger building shrouded in darkness. Rising against a starlit sky, Will saw an arch above the door where a small bell hung in dark relief from an opening in the pale adobe. "I hadn't noticed the church before," he remarked.

Father Tomas sighed. "It is the labor of many generous hands, Captain. The people of Encinal worked many years without a priest to build their church. When the bishop came and saw the fruit of their labors, he had no choice—he sent a member of the order, for how could he ignore such a sacrifice by so many poor goatherders?"

Father Tomas climbed a porch of hand-hewn cut stones to the entrance, disappearing inside. Will peered into the shadowy interior and saw a candle flickering at the feet of a statue of Mary. The priest bowed and snuffed out the flame.

"It was a sad day for the church when we buried three of our people," Isabella whispered. She stared at the darkened doorway, listening to Father Tomas's sandals sweep closer. "The funeral mass even brought tears to the eyes of Father Tomas."

Will nodded. "Worst was the boy," he sighed, when he could think of nothing better to say.

Isabella turned slowly then, looking at Will. "Your job . . . it brings you closer to death than most other men. And you must kill those who break the law."

"Sometimes," Will replied softly, remembering the battlefield littered with corpses they left behind only hours before. "Some men won't have it any other way. It comes with the job."

"I think I understand," she whispered as Father Tomas came from the church.

"And now," the priest began, "to my humble home. Two young goats are orphans and I must see to their care. A rattlesnake took the little goats' mother, and I must provide that which the serpent took away."

Father Tomas led the way through the dark, hurrying now, as if remembering the orphans reminded him of unfinished matters. A dog barked suddenly from a shadow beside an adobe, warning off the intruders until the priest silenced it with his voice. "Be silent, *perro*, for it is only Father Tomas." The dog ceased its barking and came toward the priest's shadow, wagging its tail. Father Tomas patted the dog's head and then continued on his way.

"Even the animals love him," Isabella whispered, smiling as they walked behind the quicker footsteps of Father Tomas.

Will grinned back at her, and felt her hand slip gently into the crook of his arm. "The people of your village are lucky to have this priest," Will said, not really thinking about the priest with Isabella's fingers curled around his arm. Her touch sent a tingle down the back of his neck, and his footsteps seemed lighter somehow.

At the hut Father Tomas turned and bowed. "Good night, my children. And do not forget your promise, Captain, that you will attend mass with us on Sunday."

"I haven't forgotten, Father. I'll be there, unless duty calls me away."

The old man ducked inside his hut.

"It's a nice night," Isabella said suddenly. "Walk with me to the well. A bucket of cool water will help wash the dust off my skin."

Will nodded and let the woman guide him away from the hut with gentle pressure from her hand. "I could buy a bottle of tequila," he suggested, glancing down to measure her reaction.

Isabella shook her head quickly. "I don't like the taste, Captain. Buy one for yourself if you wish."

He halted her and grinned self-consciously. "My name is Will. Calling me a captain reminds me too much of hot, dusty work."

Her smile came again. "Then Will it shall be. And you must call me Isabella."

"It's a pretty name," he said quietly. "And you're a pretty lady."

She curtsied, without letting go of his arm or taking her eyes from his face. "Thank you," she breathed, then tugging his arm toward the glitter of a stone water trough reflecting light from the stars overhead. He wondered if he were behaving as a gentleman should when in the company of a proper woman, for he was without the experience by which he might judge his actions. Proper ladies never seemed to show any interest in him, thus he'd never had the chance to practice his manners.

Beside the trough lay a circle of stones, smelling damp as they bent over to peer into the well's depths. Will sent a bucket down on a length of horsehair rope, listening to the splash.

"This well is the lifeblood of Encinal," Isabella said, as Will hoisted the bucket to the rim. "Without this water there could be no town. No one knows who dug the well, for it has been here since the time of the ancient ones. It has served many a thirsty traveler. Feel how wonderfully cool the water is."

Her hand disappeared into the bucket. Will wetted a finger. The cold water was proof of an underground spring, and had the woman not been standing there now, he would have pulled off his hat and poured the bucket over his head.

Cupping water, Isabella spread its cool wetness over her face, smiling when she noticed Will's curious stare. "It feels good at the end of a hot day," she said. She spilled a second handful across her bare chest. Will's eyes fell to the silvery trickles coursing down the gentle swells of her breasts. Damp circles appeared on her cotton blouse where the fabric covered her. Now her skin sparkled with crystal droplets, and her lips parted invitingly across perfect white teeth. Without thinking, he took a step closer and thumbed his hat brim higher as he bent down to touch her lips with his mouth.

She seemed momentarily frozen, and he wondered if she would pull away. Too, he'd forgotten about his mustache and he guessed his bristles were reason enough for her stiffness.

She pulled back and traced a fingertip over his upper lip. "It tickles." She giggled softly, then her smile faded and she tilted her face. One hand wound its way behind his neck and her lips parted. Her kiss was like velvet, and he heard a soft purr coming from her throat as her fingers tightened into his hair. He placed his hands tenderly around her waist, being careful not to crush her when his muscles tightened the embrace.

He hoped she would allow his lips to linger, but she pulled away much too soon and his heart fell. "We shouldn't do this, Captain . . . Will. My father would not approve, and the village has a thousand eyes."

He let his hands fall to his sides, keenly disappointed and at the same time tingling with excitement. She had returned his kiss, albeit briefly. It held promise of other meetings and longer kisses, if he could conduct himself as a gentleman should.

"I liked it," he whispered, hoping to form his words carefully, without knowing what to say. "You are a beautiful woman, Isabella. A man does things without thinking sometimes. Just now I couldn't help myself. If it was wrong, then I'll say I'm sorry."

She grinned. "It was not wrong, but there can be no more. Not now. Perhaps there will be another night, after I have spoken to my father. Please understand."

He shook his head, glancing around at the night shadows surrounding the well. "I reckon I'll have to wait," he replied, "but it ain't gonna be easy."

She laughed, and then surprised him by standing quickly on her tiptoes to kiss him again. He reached for her, but far too late for she had already whirled away, tossing her long mane over a shoulder in her haste.

He laughed out loud at her impulsive flirtation, drawn to it as a moth to a candle's flame. She was playing with him and his awkward show of affection, yet he discovered that he liked it and found himself strangely at ease. "If I had a rope I'd catch you like a maverick calf." He chuckled, for she had stopped a few yards away and turned to grin playfully.

She giggled. "A rope sometimes misses. Are you also a vaquero, Will?"

He shrugged. "I'm lots of things, I suppose. None of 'em are very fancy."

BLOODY SUNDAY

She thrust out her chin as if to pout. "You have many women in other towns, don't you?"

He shook his head, perhaps too quickly. "No. No other woman has ever wanted to tolerate me or my job. Rangering takes me away for some mighty long stretches."

The angle of her chin relaxed. "Would you be happy as a vaquero?" she asked softly.

He thought about his answer. He spread his palms. "I don't know, to tell the truth. I've been on the move from place to place for so long . . ."

She tossed her hair into the wind with a casual flip of her head. "Why are you a Ranger? It sounds like a lonely job."

"It gets mighty lonely sometimes. But there's times when it's peaceful, riding open range, just you and your horse under a big peaceful sky. Times, it don't seem so bad."

"Perhaps you will always be a drifter, Will? There are some men who never change."

He hooked his thumbs in his gun belt and aimed a look toward the sky. "I've been wondering, lately. I think about turning in my badge and settling down some place, only I don't know where I'd go or what I'd do. I'm a decent hand with a rope and I know horses and cattle. I'm gettin' too old to stay on the trail of outlaws and sleep with one eye open for a back-shooter. These days, it seems the gunslicks are gettin' younger and faster, and my reflexes aren't what they used to be. A man gets careless as time goes by, and then one day a bullet takes him down and it's too late to make a change."

She took a step closer, and then another, until she was in arm's reach. "And what of the men you have killed, Will? Do they come into your dreams at night to rob you of sleep?"

Her question took him by surprise, and he considered his answer. "I figure I'm doin' a job, and it's a job nobody else wants. Some folks aren't able to defend themselves. There'll always be a need for men like me who can use a gun on the right side of the law. If I go, there'll be another to take my place. It's the way of things in this hard country."

"Yes," she whispered. "Like the day Emelio Zambrano

and his bandidos came to Encinal. There must always be someone who can stop them."

She stared into Will's face, and he judged she was looking for an answer. Would he always be a drifter? For most of his life he had been on the move, and he doubted he would ever change.

"I must go now," she said, her voice trailing off. "My father will wonder where I am."

"Wish you didn't have to leave so soon," he replied, swept by urges that made him say things he hadn't said to anyone before. Isabella's beautiful face filled him with longing, a new feeling in his solitary existence up till now. He sensed a special communion between them when they looked into each other's eyes . . . it was a feeling he would be hard-pressed to explain.

"There will be other nights," she whispered. "Now I must go. I will speak to my father . . . he must approve if I am to share your company."

She turned to leave, and he reached for her, catching her waist in his big palm.

"No, Will. We mustn't," she protested, as he drew her to his chest gently yet firmly.

He bent and kissed her again, a mere brushing of his parted lips against her mouth.

"Please, Will," she whimpered softly, palms against his chest to push him away.

"Sorry," he croaked hoarsely. "Couldn't help myself."

A quick smile flashed across her face.

He released her, but to his astonishment she did not flee toward her father's store. She stood before him, staring into his eyes, and then she stood on her tiptoes again and laced her arms around his neck, pulling his face toward hers.

The crush of her mouth was warm and wonderful. He returned her pressure and heard her sigh as her body fell against his in the darkness. She clung to his neck fiercely, then she squirmed and pushed away, running as hard as she could toward the lights of town.

He listened to the patter of her sandals until the sound was lost on the night wind.

Chapter Twelve

He read the stamping on a wooden rifle crate in the first gray light of dawn. WINCHESTER REPEATING RIFLE COMPANY. MODEL 1873. Ten rifles were packed in each of the forty boxes, layered in oil and then wrapped in brown paper. Four hundred of the rifles would have been enough to turn the tide of any battle, in the right user's hands. At the front of the wagon, crates of cartridges were lashed together, enough to fuel an army in many conflicts. But not in Mexico, not with the weapons and ammunition Will saw beneath the tarp. A chance conversation overheard by a little boy led to this seizure of deadly contraband. Will wondered idly if the dead boy's mother understood just how important little Pedro's discovery had been.

He left the wagon to find a crowbar, seeking the blacksmith's as the most likely place to find such a tool. Cooking fires gave their smoke to the morning sky pinking with the fingers of dawn as Will walked to the blacksmith's shop, scattering chickens in his wake.

Passing the sleeping rooms beside the cantina, he heard Carl's snoring. Two adobe squares stood next to the cantina, serving as a hotel of sorts for the infrequent travelers to Encinal, occasional drummers peddling their wares to Ben Flowers's store, less often others coming from the east across the desert. In the morning quiet Encinal seemed an idyllic place, before the hot winds laden with dust turned the village into a chalky inferno. Will passed the darkened windows of the little shops wondering if he could be happy in Encinal. It was the woman, he decided, who made him think such thoughts . . . settling down, perhaps to raise goats like the other villagers, or a few tough-hided longhorns. It was a laughable idea, that a man bitten by wanderlust might settle in this sleepy little town for very long. Last night, still smitten by Isabella's kisses, he had been unable to sleep and thus took a turn at the watch beside the wagon, tilted back in a rawhide chair against a wagon wheel to dream foolish dreams of Isabella. But in the hard light of day he understood that he could never settle in Encinal to make her his wife, even if she agreed to the proposition. He was cut from a different cloth. The urge to saddle up and move on would eventually overtake him.

A sleepy-eyed blacksmith tended his forge, muscular arms working the bellows as Will walked beneath the thatched *ramada*. Balding, and already sweating from his labors, the blacksmith looked up and halted his bellows.

"I need an iron bar to open a crate," Will said.

"You aim to have a look at them rifles?" he asked, turning from his forge, scowling into a toolbox.

Will guessed everyone in the village had heard about the guns. "Just one box. Curiosity, mostly."

"Help yourself, Ranger," he replied, handing Will a flat bar with a nail-clawed end. "We're mighty damn grateful for what you and your men done the other day. I saw the fight from my bedroom window. You fellers can damn sure shoot. The name's Sikes. Folks mostly call me Big John."

He stuck out his hand and Will took it. In his prime Sikes had been an uncommonly strong man. His arms bore the scars of his profession, working heated metal. "I'll bring the harness teams over," Will offered. "They made a long haul from Kansas and a couple of 'em may need new iron."

Sikes nodded. "Appreciate the business. I'll look them over."

Will started back to the wagon cradling the bar as the eastern sky turned golden. As if given a signal, the goats began to bleat in a swelling chorus. Dogs barked, and then there was the tinkle of a lead goat's bell in the distance. Cotton-clad boys ran to the goat pens, shouldering gourds of water. Others led reluctant burros from thatched shelters. A building wind carried the scent of frying tortillas and goat meat. Smoke from the cooking fires now bent sharply away from chimneys, swept by the winds.

He tossed the tarp aside and lowered the tailgate. A boot scraped behind him, and out of old habit his right hand went quickly to the butt of his gun.

"It's me, Cap'n," he heard Billy say.

His hand relaxed, for he knew the voice. Had it been an enemy, he would have been kneeling in the dirt just now, clutching a mortal wound. He cursed his carelessness silently. "Got my mind on that woman," he muttered, pulling a rifle crate to the back of the wagon.

He pried open the lid and set the tool aside to remove one of the paper-wrapped guns. Oily film covered his fingers as he took the wrapping off.

"Eighteen seventy-three," Billy observed over Will's shoulder. "Older model. I don't reckon a Mexican cares, if it'll shoot."

The new rifle gleamed with its layer of grease. "It's good enough to fight a revolution," Will declared.

"Folks somewhere will be glad they didn't fall into Zambrano's hands," Billy added.

Will wrapped the rifle in its paper and closed the wooden lid. "These guns cost a feller by the name of Ortega a small fortune. Tom Hickok won't be welcome south of the border for a spell. He took the money and never made his delivery. If I was wearin' Hickok's boots, I'd be headed back to Dodge City quick as I could."

"He's lucky he ain't in a pine box," Billy said. "Carl had ol' Betsy's barrels heated up in that river."

Will remembered the gun battle with no particular satisfaction. It had been necessary, to keep Hickok and his deputies from taking Leon to Colonel Diaz. "There's been a drop or two of blood shed over these guns," Will agreed.

"You figure it's over?" Billy asked quietly.

Will gazed at the southern horizon. "Zambrano won't come back now. He lost too many men. He knows he'd have to raise an army to get his hands on the rifles. We'll have a quiet ride to San Antone."

"There's some who say otherwise," Billy warned. "The old bartender acts worried. He claims Zambrano is near 'bout famous over in Mexico for being good with a gun. Arturo thinks he'll come back to settle the score with us."

Something Travis Hollaman said awakened in Will's memory. "Captain Hollaman said Zambrano was dangerous. A man's reputation gets blown up sometimes. Maybe he was just lucky up till now."

Billy nodded like he understood. "A few years back it got to where I couldn't ride into a town without having some green kid call me out. The more of them you kill, the bigger your reputation gets, only you know down inside that they were just little boys who talked big. Wasn't none of them who could hit the side of a barn. I got me a bellyful of it, Will. Huntin' men for bounty is a lighted fuse . . . you've only got just so much time."

"Workin' for the Rangers can be the same, Billy. A man gets old doin' the job, and his gun hand gets slower."

"You figurin' on hanging it up?" Billy asked.

Will sighed, slumping against a wagon wheel. "It's run through my mind lately."

"Is it that woman?"

Will chuckled softly and shook his head. "I ain't the marrying kind. I was born with this itch in my britches to move around when I take the notion. A woman could never understand it."

"She's pretty, Will. Maybe you'd see things different if you tried it for a spell."

Will let it drop, for the tingle returned in the pit of his stomach when he thought about Isabella. He knew he was too old and too set in his ways to change, but as he thought about last night's embraces under the stars, he found himself wondering if an old dog could learn new tricks.

By the middle of the morning the heat and the wind had driven everyone into the shade. Will and Billy and Carl sat in the cantina, listening to John Sikes pound his anvil at the north end of town where Leon had taken the harness horses to have their hooves attended. Will nursed a glass of tequila, following a breakfast of tortillas and eggs, thinking vaguely pleasant thoughts of Isabella and her playful flirting. She had spoken to him on her way to the store this morning, but only a greeting. He wondered if she regretted last night's brief encounter.

About noon he heard a commotion outside, the laughing of many small children, and to pass the time he got up and left the cantina to watch the children play. But he found that the children were not at play, instead seated around Father Tomas in the shade of a big mesquite.

"Book," the priest cried, grinning as he held his bible aloft. "*En Ingles* . . . a book!"

"Book!" the children shouted. More than a dozen small brown faces watched Father Tomas intently.

"Again, it is . . . a book."

"A book," the children echoed in a single voice.

Then Father Tomas noticed Will, and he beckoned him closer. Will shrugged and started across the street, hat tilted into the wind. A black dog growled as he approached the children.

"Welcome to our school," the priest beamed. "My students are learning English." He turned to the children and pointed to Will. "*Capitan de los* Rangers."

Almond eyes widened among the children. There were no smiles, and on some of the faces Will saw fear.

"They're afraid of me," Will said softly.

Father Tomas shook his head. "It is your gun that they fear, Captain. I took all the children and made them stand near the bodies of the bandits in front of the cantina. I wanted them to see for themselves what guns do to men. It was a lesson, of just as much importance as learning to read. They must be made to understand that guns are evil, so no more children will lose their lives the way little Pedro Morales lost his. The boy was drawn to the wicked bandits, fascinated by their guns and the stories told about this terrible Zambrano!

He would not listen to me, and now his precious life is ended by a simple boy's curiosity. But these children were made to look at the dead you left behind . . . I wanted them to understand that a gun is not a toy."

He looked around the group when the priest was finished, wishing for a way to explain what the Rangers had done. "You need to teach them that there are times when a gun is necessary, Father."

Father Tomas shook his head. "Life for them is a bitter struggle, my son," he said softly. "In the hands of these simple people, a gun will only get them killed. It is enough that they must survive the dry years, the coyotes feeding on their goats, and the rattlesnakes. For these children, a gun is useless."

Will turned on his heel and started back across the road, supposing as he went that the priest's logic befit the lives of the people of Encinal. Goatherders didn't need guns and probably couldn't be taught how to use them . . . all the more reason why there must be men like himself to protect them.

He saw Ben Flowers heading down the street in his direction, face bent, hurrying his strides. Will tried to guess his purpose as the storekeeper drew near. Pink-faced, Isabella's father came to an abrupt halt in front of Will and placed his hands on his hips.

"You've got no business toying with my daughter's affections," Ben snapped. "And you're much too old for her, Captain Dobbs."

Ben's eyes betrayed him—his words were angry, but his gaze flickered, uncertain.

"I'm not toying with her at all," Will replied gently. "I enjoy her company. She's a beautiful woman."

"She's much too young," Ben persisted, unable to look Will squarely in the eye. "She asked for my permission to spend some time with you. I won't give it! She's still a child."

"I never asked her her age," Will said. "We seemed to share an attraction—if that's the right word. I liked her the minute I saw her. We just went for a walk last night. She showed me the well."

Ben's face furrowed more deeply. "She's only nineteen, and you're twice her age. Good grief, Captain—don't you have any sort of conscience?"

"I've done nothing wrong," Will replied evenly, "and I didn't know age was so all-fired important. Isabella is a beautiful woman. Any man will look twice when he sees her the first time."

It seemed Ben's shoulders sagged. Face downcast, he shook his head. "That's the trouble—she's too beautiful. Hardly a cowboy or a drummer comes to town without staring at her. She looks like her mother. Ah, but her mother was a dark-eyed Spanish beauty to behold."

"You said, 'was'?" Will repeated.

"Her mother died of the consumption six years ago, and I'm left with the job of raising a daughter by myself." He sighed. "Nineteen is so young."

"You have nothing to fear from me," Will said. "I won't be taking your daughter away from you, if that's what has got you worried. And I won't do her any harm. Truth is, I enjoy her company, and it appears she enjoys mine. You've got your tail tied in a knot over nothing."

Ben looked up then and his face was changed. "I'm relieved, Captain. I'm sure you know that some men are without honorable intentions. . . . Some might try to . . . force themselves on an innocent young girl like Isabella. I'm sorry for what I said. Sorry for the way I said it. The people of this town owe you a great debt, and I let my jealous nature get the best of me, I suppose. I love my daughter, and she's all I have left. Maybe I've tried to protect her too much. . . ."

"You've got nothing to worry about from me. I reckon you could say I've got honorable intentions when it comes to your daughter . . . just sharing a few minutes of her company. We'll be pulling out tomorrow with the wagon. Odds are, you and Isabella will never see me again."

"Sorry, Captain," Ben said again, looking down at his shoes. "I had it figured wrong. Tonight, after we close the store, I'd like to invite you to our home for supper. Maybe that'll mend a busted fence."

"No fence has been cut," Will replied, looking past the storekeeper as Leon led the four harness horses from the blacksmith. "No need to go to all that trouble."

"It's no trouble," Ben protested, but Will had already turned away to lend Leon a hand with the horses, walking toward the livery as wind gusted around him, fluttering his hat brim and duster.

Chapter Thirteen

He gathered his men around him at dusk to issue a stern warning; all afternoon he watched the southern horizon with a vague uneasiness. Tom Hickok was his main concern. "Keep an eye on the wagon," Will said, shifting his weight from one foot to another. "Those rifles are too valuable for a greedy man to ignore. It's Hickok I'm worried about— those men he hired to guard the guns are in Laredo. If they get the wounded to Doc Warren and then happen to run across Hickok . . ."

He needn't finish to satisfy Leon and Billy. Carl seemed puzzled. "They was whupped men, Cap'n," Carl remarked. "I don't figure they'll show themselves around here again. A man who tastes lead ain't got much fight left in him."

"Just the same, I want a guard on that wagon tonight," Will said, aiming a thumb over his shoulder. Evening shadows turned plum purple on the hills south of Encinal. Spiked cholla and yucca bristled against the darkening sky. Will studied the land and felt a growing sense of forboding . . . something was wrong out there. He could almost feel it in his fingertips.

He left the front of the cantina to walk farther south, to the edge of the desert, perhaps to better understand what was making him edgy. Whitewing doves fluttered from his path, making their gentle sounds moving from limb to limb in the dense mesquites as he left the outskirts of Encinal to enter the brush beside the wagon road. *Chichadas* buzzed away from him, snapping like brittle branches, leaving their resting places. An owl hooted once, then again. His boots crunched into the thorns and dry stalks, spurs tinkling of metal, harsh and yet not out of place with their sharp rowels. When he reached a mound of empty caliche he stopped to listen to the desert. A coyote barked somewhere, adding its song to the coming night.

He faced the wind and sniffed its fragrances—the acrid scent of sappy mesquite and a hint of dust. Crimson sprays reached skyward from the setting sun, painting a cloudless horizon red with its rays of light. He knew something was wrong beyond the slope of the earth before him . . . he could almost reach out and touch its ugliness. His stomach knotted. Sweat came to his palms and he thought he must be feeling the vibrations of Mother Earth, like an Indian. Comanches believed in messages from the Spirit World, revealed in earthly signs—the flight of an eagle or the lifted tail of a doe when it faced the sun. A white man could never understand spirit signs, but now Will wondered if he were being given a sign by forces he could not comprehend.

"Maybe it's just old age," he told himself, sighting along the horizon. The hills to the south of Encinal were empty, and he puzzled over his uneasiness. Earlier in the day he'd been sure the trouble over the guns was at an end. Now, something gnawed away at him, knotted in the pit of his stomach.

A velvety curtain of darkness moved across the prairie as the last rays of the sun purpled, then grayed. Stars blinked above the silent hills. Will glanced down the Laredo road before he left the caliche mound. Thorns clawed his denims in the tightly-packed brush. Head down, he walked to the wagon ruts and headed for the cantina, deciding on a bottle of tequila as a remedy for his concerns.

Carl saw him approach, leaning against a wagon wheel. "What's eating on you, Cap'n?"

Will cast a look over his shoulder. "I wish I knew. Old age, I reckon." He saw the bottle in Carl's fist. "Don't let that agave juice make you careless. Keep your eyes peeled."

He entered the cantina and found it empty. Arturo was in the kitchen banging pans together, his shadow moving across the floor when he passed beneath the lantern. Will took a fresh bottle of tequila from a shelf behind the bar and uncorked it. His spurs alerted Arturo; the bartender's head peered around the door frame, and Will saw a question on his face.

"Only me," Will said, dropping a coin on the bar.

Arturo nodded. "Your *compadres*, they sleep."

Will guessed that Billy and Leon had departed for the small rooms. He waved to Arturo and walked back outside where Carl lounged beside the wagon. Across the village the goats were begging for food and water. Lanterns came to life behind windows in the huts.

"Peaceful little place, ain't it?" Carl asked, watching a young boy urge his burro between the adobes. "Biggest worry they've got is a well running dry."

"Maybe," Will said, looking south again.

"If I was you, Cap'n, I'd ask that pretty woman to marry me and I'd find me a place to settle down . . . maybe a place like this, only cooler in the summer. I'd buy a few cows and take life easy. I'd do it, if I got the chance."

Will glanced toward the store and the porch where yesterday Isabella had been sweeping. No lights burned behind the windows. The store had closed early, and he supposed it was because today was Saturday. "You make it sound mighty inviting, Carl. Trouble is, the pretty lady wouldn't marry me if I asked." He felt Carl's gaze and turned toward him.

"You're wrong, Cap'n. That woman has got eyes for you, only you're too damn blind to see it."

He heard the soft whisper of sandaled feet. A shadow came toward them from the darkness, and he saw the flutter of a woman's skirt in the wind. Light from the cantina windows brightened the figure and then he heard Carl chuckle softly.

"Like I said, Cap'n, you're goin' blind."

Isabella's smile warmed him, relaxing the knot in his belly. "Good evening, Will," she said, halting in a square of light. Her soft hair caressed her bare shoulders. A pale yellow blouse revealed more of her than yesterday. A white skirt clung to her thighs in the wind.

"Good evening, Isabella. You look prettier than ever."

She glanced uncertainly at Carl. "My father and I invite you to our house. Please come."

He shook his head, remembering Ben Flowers's concerns. "I'd better stay close to the wagon, but thanks anyway."

Her wonderful smile waned, and Will was immediately sorry.

"It's okay, Cap'n," Carl said. "I'll keep an eye on the guns. If you hear ol' Betsy bark, then come a-runnin'."

He commenced an argument with himself while Isabella watched him expectantly. He didn't want further entanglements with the woman, tempting him to think of himself in a quieter life as a settled man. He understood himself too well—he could never be a respectable husband who stayed in one place to raise a family. Being with Isabella raised his expectations, making him think he stood a chance of winning her affections, knowing all the while that he wasn't suited for permanence. But when he looked at her now, knowing all these things about himself and his chances, his resolve melted. "I reckon I can spare a few minutes," he said.

She took his hand and pulled him away from the cantina, and he knew Carl was watching as they walked side by side across the road. "My father told me that he spoke with you today," Isabella whispered. "He was angry right at first, when I asked him if we could spend some time together."

She squeezed his hand and his arm tingled. "He wasn't very happy with the idea," Will replied, as a gust of wind swirled about them."

"He thinks you plan to carry me off." Isabella giggled. They rounded a turn and walked past the livery. Suddenly she stopped short and faced him in the starlight. "Is that your plan, Captain Will Dobbs?" she asked softly. "Will you carry me away to San Antonio?"

Her eyes sparkled, and he wondered if she wanted a serious answer. He grinned. "Maybe. Would you go?"

Her face tilted coyly and her smile broadened. "Perhaps. You haven't asked."

He was thankful for the dark, for he knew his cheeks were

coloring. "Maybe I will. If I thought the idea would make you happy . . ."

His voice trailed off. He'd said more than he intended. Isabella squeezed his palm again and something fluttered inside his chest.

She seemed about to speak, then thought better of it and tugged him away from the stable. "Supper is waiting," she explained, hurrying him toward a lamplit adobe.

He removed his hat in gentlemanly fashion when he entered the front room. The little house was clean; whitewashed walls bore handmade decorations, paper flowers and deer antlers strung with colored beads. Ben Flowers came from the kitchen when he heard Will's boots. He nodded politely and pointed to a bull-hide chair.

"Take a seat, Captain. I've been saving some good brandy for a special occasion." He took a bottle from a shelf and began to pour.

Will shouldered out of his duster and hung it on a peg. His hat went over the coat before he took the chair. Ben handed him a glass of sweet-smelling brandy and took a chair opposite Will.

"Glad you came," Ben remarked as Isabella disappeared into the kitchen. Wonderful smells floated from the doorway, hinting of spices and warm tortillas and *cebolla* onions. "I was hoping that what I said wouldn't keep you away."

Will sipped brandy and shook his head. "I never had a daughter, so I can only guess that I'd hand the same speech to any man who winked at her."

Ben sighed, glancing over his shoulder once before he spoke again. "Isabella is a lovely girl and I want the best for her. Encinal is no place for a young woman. This town is always going to be a hardscrabble existence. I want my daughter to have more from life than this . . . I want her to be happy."

Will started to speak, bethought himself and let it pass. Ben was trying to make his apology for angry words said earlier in the day.

"Come," Isabella said from the kitchen doorway.

Will downed his brandy and pushed out of the chair to follow Ben into the next room. A small table sat near one wall, laden with steaming bowls and platters of tortillas. A washbasin rested on a counter beside the back door. Will poured water on his hands and toweled them dry.

Isabella showed him to a chair and removed her white apron. "Sit here, Captain," she said with unexpected formality. His glance fell to the cleft of her bosom as she seated herself. Reminded of her father's presence, he turned his attention to the table.

They ate spicey goat meat and frijoles, beans swimming in juice speckled with cilantro and bits of onion. Always mindful of his manners, he tried to chew with his mouth closed and without slurping from his spoon. All the while he felt Isabella's eyes on him. He squirmed in his hide-bottom chair when her glances stayed too long.

The meal ended with cups of flan, thick with browned sugar syrup. Will tried to eat slowly in spite of the delicious taste. Ben seemed unaware of the looks his daughter gave Will across the table; his face was bent over his plate and he did not utter a word until his plate was empty.

"It was delicious," Will said when the last of his flan was gone. "I hadn't eaten a home-cooked meal in a long time."

Isabella bowed as she cleaned plates from the table. "I am pleased that you liked it, Captain," she replied.

Ben shoved his chair back. "I've got a box of cigars in the front room. We can sit on the porch, where it's cooler."

Will thought he saw a look of shared conspiracy in Isabella's eyes. "I will need a bucket of fresh water from the well to clean our dishes," she said. "Perhaps Captain Dobbs will be kind enough to draw water for me, when you are finished with your cigars."

Ben grunted agreement and walked into the front room. "Have a cigar," he said, offering a box. He struck a match to their smokes and walked outside where a cool breeze rattled drying gourds hung from a porch beam.

They sat on a bench and smoked in silence. The rattle of

plates came the kitchen, and to the east they heard the bleating of kid goats searching for milk.

"I worry about those damn guns," Ben said unexpectedly. "I'll be glad when you get them away from Encinal. Emelio Zambrano is a bloody cutthroat. I don't want him back in this town."

"We're leaving in the morning for San Antone," Will said. "I promised Father Tomas that I'd stay for mass tomorrow."

Ben flicked ashes from his cigar; orange sparks drifted northeast on the wind. "Father Tomas has exacted his price, I gather?" Ben chuckled. "He is wonderful with the children. We have no school, but the priest teaches the little ones on special days. We are fortunate to have him here. And because of him, we have the miracle of a telegraph."

Will nodded. "That warning the priest sent when Zambrano came probably saved many lives."

"I feared that they would kill us all," Ben said, reflecting on the bandits' arrival. "They made a game of it . . . shooting at our feet when we left our houses. And there was poor Sanches, and Ben Wheeler, and the boy. *Dios*, why did little Pedro go to the cantina that day? Now, his mother dies slowly of grief."

"A boy grows fascinated with guns sometimes," Will remarked, remembering his own youth on the Middle Bosque hunting squirrels with an ancient shotgun. "Some men never lose the interest. I couldn't wait to go off to war when I turned seventeen. I didn't know what the bleeding and dying would be like. I did a bunch of growing up when I saw what a gun did to soldiers."

"The corpses you left behind in Encinal were no different, Captain. What a bloody mess to bury."

Will agreed without comment. More corpses lay two hours west of Encinal, left to rot in the summer sun. There had been enough bloodshed over one wagonload of rifles. He would be glad when the drive to San Antonio put the business to rest.

Isabella appeared on the porch carrying a bucket. "Will you help me with the water, Captain?" she asked.

He stood up and ground out the stub of his cigar, wondering if Ben was wise to the ruse. "Glad to help," he said softly, taking the bucket from Isabella's slender fingers.

"Wake me in time for mass, Isabella," Ben called from the porch. "I'm turning in. Good night, Captain Dobbs."

They walked side by side into the darkness, aiming for the goat pens and the sheltering trees above the well. When they were safely away from the house, Isabella found Will's hand and clasped it in hers, squeezing it gently.

"It was so hot in the kitchen," she said. "The water from the well will feel good tonight. I brought a gourd sponge so I can wash the dust from my skin, but you will have to promise me that you will turn your back until I am finished."

A thrill of excitement shortened Will's steps. Just the thought of Isabella's naked body glistening with water made his mouth run dry. His heart beat faster. "I'll try," he said, as sincerely as he could under the circumstances.

She giggled and held back, still clinging to his hand. "I must have your word that your back will be turned."

He nodded and pulled her along toward the well, enjoying her playful suggestion that his first answer was not good enough. "I'm a man, Isabella," he replied, "but I'll do my best. You've got my word on that."

They came to the well and discovered two cotton-clad boys lifting a bucket from its depths. Both boys spoke to Isabella, darting quick looks Will's way before they hurried off with the bucket slopping water noisily around its sides.

"It is still early," Isabella whispered, gazing up at the stars. "Leave the bucket here and we will walk to the top of the hill. You can see for many miles . . . we follow the goat trail to the top."

She led him away from the well, into the waist-high mesquite and brittle brush, wind tossing her hair about her face and neck as they wound along a footpath beaten to powder by a thousand cloven hooves. The trail led up a gentle rise, to a clearing at the top of the knoll where salt licks lay scattered, dished to a hollow by the goats' tongues.

Isabella turned abruptly and stood on her toes to kiss him, a quick peck below his mustache. "Here, no one can see us," she whispered.

Her face tilted up towards his and a question filled her eyes. "Tomorrow you leave Encinal," she whispered. "Will I ever see you again?"

He shook his head, forming his answer. "My job keeps me on the move, but I promise I'll come back." Then he chewed his lip and sought a better explanation. "I've been thinking about leaving the Texas Rangers . . . maybe going into the cattle business. I've got a little money saved. It won't be enough, but it's a start. After I get those guns safe to San Antone, I aim to do a little lookin' around for a small place where I could run a few cows."

She pulled her arms from his neck and stepped back. Her face was serious, eyes dark with concern. "And what if you find a place to raise your cows?" she asked.

He took a deep breath and considered his answer very carefully. "I'm liable to ride down to Encinal and ask you to marry me, Isabella. I'm not rightly sure I'm cut out for that kind of life, but I might give it a try."

She studied his face for a while, and he could see that her eyes were clouded by thought. He didn't know what else to say and the result was silence. Isabella slowly lifted a hand to pull a stray lock of hair from her forehead without looking from Will's face.

"My heart wants to believe you," she whispered. "I guess I'll have to wait and see if you return."

He shifted his weight uncomfortably. "Will you be here?" he asked, toeing the ground with a boot.

A slow smile crossed her face. "I guess you'll have to wait and see. Now come. Let's go back to the well."

She hurried past him and started down the trail on her own. He followed, rattling his spurs, wondering if Isabella would marry him should he ask the question directly.

Darkened windows around the village warned that the hour

was late. Now the goats were silent in the pens and no villagers walked about. Reaching the well, he sent the bucket down. Isabella stood beside him in the deeper shadows beneath the trees.

He looked at her as he brought the bucket to the top. She smiled, and his heart quickened. He poured the water into her bucket and turned to leave, thinking some dark worry held her tongue.

She removed a small gourd sponge from a pocket of her skirt and soaked it in the bucket. First she passed the sponge over her cheeks, closing her eyes contentedly as the cool water crossed her skin. Another spongeful wetted her neck and shoulders with gentle pats. "It feels good," she whispered dreamily. "Now turn your back, and promise me you won't turn around."

A grin wrinkled his features. "It'll be a powerful temptation, but you've got my word."

He swung his back to her and heard the soft rustle of fabric.

Water bubbled in the bucket, and Will took a deep breath. A few drops tinkled to the surface and then there was silence. "I wish you'd let me turn around," he whispered. "You're the most beautiful woman I ever met in my life, and I can't believe I'm not looking at you every chance I get. I must be part fool to stand here like this. You strike a hard bargain, Isabella."

Water dribbled into the bucket again and he could hear the sponge crossing her skin. He swallowed.

"You promised," she said quietly.

"Yeah. And I'm the fool for it."

He flinched when he felt her hand on his shoulder. "Now you may turn around, Captain Dobbs."

As he turned he saw her yellow blouse and white skirt lying across the circle of stones around the well. Then he saw Isabella in the shadows and his heart stopped beating altogether.

Chapter Fourteen

He sat up on the rawhide-bottom cot and blinked once. Pale gray sky lighted the window. Swinging his feet to the floor, he cleared away the cobwebs of sleep to focus his thoughts on the day before him. A grin creased his face as a recollection of last night's intimacy with Isabella returned. Soft skin and quiet murmurs under the stars had sealed his fate as surely as if he were hog-tied. He had never known another woman like Isabella . . . never beheld such physical perfection or dreamed it possible. It was a stroke of incredible good fortune that she was attracted to him. Like a doomed man headed for the gallows, he knew his days as a Ranger were numbered. He would ride back to Encinal and ask Isabella to marry him when the rifles were safely in San Antonio.

The rifles. He remembered his dark worries yesterday, that Tom Hickok would come to Encinal to make a try for the guns. The night had passed without incident, disproving the subtle stirring of his senses warning of trouble. There was still a hundred miles of rough terrain to cross with the wagon, yet it appeared that his guess had been wrong about Hickok. Dawn had come peacefully to Encinal.

He got up slowly to splash water on his face from a basin on a table beside the cot. A filmy piece of mirror hung on the wall, and he set about to shave his stubble before it, grinding a dull razor over his cheeks. A rooster crowed somewhere in the village, announcing the new day—Sunday. He had promised to attend mass before they left with the wagon, and he would keep the promise, for no better reason than to show Isabella that he was a man of his word.

He pulled on the gray shirt and noted the missing buttons. If things worked out, there would be someone to do his mending in the days to come. He grinned at his reflection. "You're about to be tamed, Will Dobbs. Your wild oats have gone to seed."

He strapped on his gun and sleeved into the duster, adding his hat to his attire before he swung back the thin plank door.

Billy raised a hand in silent greeting as Will walked out of the sleeping room shouldering his saddlebags and rifle. Goats heralded the coming day with their pitiful bleating as Will headed toward the wagon on stiffened knees.

"It's Sunday," Will observed, tossing his gear beside a wagon wheel. "Time we headed north. I had it figured wrong, looks like. I've been expecting Tom Hickok to make one more play to get his hands on those rifles."

Billy squinted toward the southern hills bathed in golden sunlight. Shadows paled below the yucca and gnarled mesquites. Wind tossed the slender mesquite leaves about like beckoning fingers, rattling the dry beans. "Most everyone else is worried about Zambrano," Billy said, sweeping the horizon. "The old bartender acts as nervous as a tomcat under a rocking chair. Maybe Carl is right—they had their asses whipped and don't want any more of us."

Old feelings returned when Will gazed south. He tried to put them aside. "Reputation makes some men seem bigger. Folks in these parts have listened to all those stories about Zambrano. I had Hickok pegged for the gent who would stir the pot. He was mighty damn sure of himself in Laredo. Looks like he can't raise enough gunhands to make a play."

Billy inclined his head toward the wagon. "We ain't made it to San Antone just yet, Will. I never was one to count chickens until I saw the eggs."

Will nodded. "You're dead right . . . we've got a long road ahead of us, across some mighty empty country. There's a hundred places where a bunch of owlhoots could jump us. We'll need to keep our eyes open."

"You could hang that badge back on Leon," Billy declared. "Leon makes a fight less worrisome."

"I can't do that and I've already said my piece on it. I can't do it and that's my last word. Leon can ride along and I'm pleased to have his company, but he don't wear a badge."

"I won't mention it again," Billy replied. "Let's see if Arturo has boiled any coffee, then I'll get the harness and start hitchin' up the teams."

"No particular hurry," Will sighed, turning his gaze from the hills. "I promised the old priest that I'd go to church this morning. It's what he wanted for sending the wire to Laredo."

He caught Billy grinning as they entered the cantina. "That gal has got you roped and branded, Cap'n. First off, she got you taking regular baths, and now she's headed you to a church. Carl had it figured right all along—you've come down with a touch of woman-fever."

Will ignored Billy's needling and went to the kitchen, following the scent of coffee. Arturo was laboring over his iron stove, feeding the fire with sticks of dry mesquite. A smoke-blackened coffeepot bubbled softly.

"Smells about ready," Will suggested, taking a tin cup.

When Arturo turned from his stove Will noted that the old man's hands were trembling.

"Anything wrong?" Will asked.

Arturo bowed his head and quickly crossed himself, eyes tightly closed. As it was Sunday, the gesture didn't seem out of place until the old man spoke. "Today will be a black day in Encinal," he whispered, tossing a glance toward the back door. "He is coming, señor. My spirit has heard his footsteps in a dream."

Will searched Arturo's face. "Who is coming, old man?"

Arturo's eyes widened. He swallowed once. "Zambrano!" he croaked, strangling on the name.

"You know this from a dream?"

Arturo shook his head. "His footsteps awakened me."

Will formed an argument, until he remembered his own vague uneasiness the day before. Something was troubling the old man, most likely a lifetime habit of superstitious belief in dreams and ghosts and miracles. Had Arturo sensed the same ominous shift in the winds that had kept him on edge the day before?

Will poured two cups of coffee while Arturo rolled balls of dough for tortillas, deciding it was best to say nothing to the old man about his dreams. Arturo would believe what he wanted anyway, and until the wagon rolled out of Encinal, nothing would convince him that the black day he predicted would not come to pass.

Carl and Leon joined them outside half an hour later, after the little church bell sounded announcing the mass. Carl's eyes were bloodshot and his mood was ugly after a bout with too much tequila. Leon piled their gear beside the wagon, balancing his Winchester in one hand as he went across the road to fork hay for the horses.

Will sighed, downing the last of his coffee. "Time I kept my promise and went to church."

"Don't let that preacher get you hitched to the pretty gal while you're dozin'." Carl chuckled. "Not unless you're ready to trade that dun horse for a rocking chair and some knittin' needles."

Will trudged away, following scattered groups of people toward the church, ignoring Carl's remark. He saw Isabella and her father, walking arm in arm between the adobes. Ben was clad in a black broadcloth suit and bow tie. Isabella wore a flowing green dress. A matching ribbon decorated her hair. Isabella was watching him as he strode for the church. A smile crossed her face and she waved, speaking to her father.

People dressed in their Sunday best formed a line into the church, bowing to Father Tomas as they crossed the threshold into the building. Father Tomas wore a soft white robe, clasped about his middle by a length of satin rope. The priest saw Will and nodded his approval as Will joined Isabella and her father at the back of the waiting line.

"Good morning," the priest intoned, smiling broadly when Ben guided Isabella up the steps. Will had mumbled "good morning" to Isabella and her father, strangely self-conscious after last night's intimacy with Ben's daughter. Isabella seemed to sense his discomfort. She lowered her face and remained silent as they walked up the steps to greet the priest.

"And good morning to you, Captain Dobbs. You kept your promise, and now your debt is paid," Father Tomas assured. "I won't keep you long. The mass is short."

They entered the church and stood, for there were no benches or chairs. An altar of mortared stones stood at the front of the room. A brass cup sat between two flickering candles on the altar. A sculpture of the Virgin Mary sat in an alcove to one side of the altar. On the wall hung a wooden relief of Jesus on His cross. Unaccustomed as Will was to the insides of churches, he'd forgotten to remove his hat until a stern look from Isabella served as a reminder. She smiled briefly as he pulled off his hat, then she looked away.

Fifty or sixty people crowded the room, women and children in spotless white homespun, and men in loose-fitted cotton pants and shapeless shirts cut from flour sacking. Big John Sikes stood in front of Will, his bald head gleaming in the candle's glow. He recognized one or two more, a tall youth named Paulito, who had helped repair the telegraph wire, and a stocky goatherder called Juan, who came to the cantina for an occasional shot of pulque. Other faces looked vaguely familiar, without names he remembered.

Father Tomas came slowly down an aisle toward the front of the church, reading from his bible. Will clasped his hat brim and listened patiently.

The little church grew hot as the minutes passed with Father Tomas reading, his monotone beating rhythmically, accompanied only by the sighing of the wind through the trees beyond the church. Beads of sweat formed down Will's back and on his forehead. He sleeved the sweat from his face and rocked once on his boot heels.

Then Father Tomas ended his reading and took a cup of bits of bread to the first row of worshipers. Speaking softly, he passed among them. Each bowed when the bread was given. Will watched and grew restless.

A sound distracted him—metal rattling against metal—and he turned to look over his shoulder, frowning, for the sound was familiar and yet he had trouble identifying it quickly. He heard it again, moving closer, and now he knew the sound; someone was running in booted feet, rattling spurs.

"Cap'n! Cap'n! Come quick!" a voice cried. It was Leon's voice and its urgency puzzled him. Isabella heard it, too, and she glanced over at Will, questioning him with her eyes.

The rattling spurs clanked heavily on the stone steps leading into the church. Father Tomas looked up but did not stop his soft-voiced blessings. Leon's shadow fell on the floor of the church and Will turned, curling his hat brim in an unconscious fist.

"Zambrano!" Leon shouted into the bowels of the church, his face turned to Will. "Hurry, Cap'n! Zambrano is coming!"

First there were whispers. Father Tomas fell silent. Then a scream shattered the quiet and Pedro Morales's mother collapsed on the hard stone floor. Will started forward as more screams echoed off the adobe walls. He bumped into a shrieking woman and knocked her aside as he ran to the door of the church.

"Look yonder, Cap'n," Leon cried, pointing south.

At first Will saw nothing but empty prairie—brush-choked hills and wind-tossed mesquite limbs. Then suddenly his eyes focused and he saw a line of tiny specks on the horizon. He shielded his eyes with a hand to block out the sun and squinted at the distant specks. Dust swirled behind the moving horses. Will's gaze moved up and down the line of mounted men spread across the southern hills.

"Must be fifty or more," Leon insisted. "Could be seventy-five if a man could get 'em still long enough to count. Four or five run their horses mighty hard to the north, around town. I figure they're headed to the telegraph wire, afore we can get word to San Antone."

Will was jostled by moving bodies as people ran from the church. Some were crying, the women and children. Men pointed to the advancing riders, chattering in rapid Spanish.

"How can you tell it's Zambrano?" Will asked quickly, trying to form a plan against tremendous odds.

"The bunch that rode around town was wearin' sombreros, Cap'n. Looks like Zambrano gathered up those revolutionaries to come and claim their guns."

Will bolted off the steps, running as hard as he could for the cantina. "Too many!" he cried when Leon ran up beside him. "We haven't got a chance against a bunch that big."

Leon swung a look south. "Billy is breakin' out the rifles and ammunition. Maybe some of these Mexicans can shoot."

Will's feet skidded to a halt. "Get the rifles off that wagon and haul them inside the cantina," he ordered. "I forgot about that telegraph. It's our only chance to get help. I'll round up any of the villagers who can shoot and bring them along, but first I've got to get the priest to that telegraph."

"Yessir, Cap'n," Leon shouted, running again toward the wagon where Billy and Carl tossed wooden crates to the ground as fast as they could.

Will wheeled and ran back for the steps, where a cluster of people stood around Father Tomas. Ben and Isabella hurried toward him, Isabella lifting her green dress to allow for running. "Get to the cantina," he cried. "I've got to send a wire before the bandits cut it down."

Father Tomas saw Will and he seemed to understand at once. He hurried off the steps, fumbling for his key.

"There isn't much time, Father," Will shouted as the men met. "Get that telegraph going. Tell them bandits are across the border again, and Captain Will Dobbs requests a platoon of soldiers!"

The priest nodded, running as fast as his robe would permit toward the telegraph office. Will broke off and headed for the cantina, his heart pounding now, for he could see the mounted men clearly beneath the wavering cloud of dust. Sombreros were silhouetted against the morning sky, spread across the southern horizon like an invading army.

"We'll never hold them back," Will told himself, trotting to the wagon. "Too damn many this time. We waited too long, and it's my fault on account of that damn promise to the priest!"

Encinal had come alive with running feet and shouting voices. Fear drove people to confusion—some ran back and forth aimlessly, screaming in Spanish, eyes wide with the terror of Zambrano's return. *"Dios! Dios!"* a cry echoed from a tear-choked woman. She stumbled in her blind haste and went sprawling on her face in the caliche road.

Carl looked up when Will arrived, a crate of ammunition poised in his hands. "We're in for one hell of a fight, Cap'n," he snarled around the stump of a cigar. "Gonna be a lot of Meskin blood gets spilled. Reckon any of these damn sheepherders can shoot?"

Ben was helping with the crates of rifles, carrying a heavy box into the cantina, in his shirtsleeves now. Will could not find Isabella in the noise and confusion. He beckoned to Ben as the storekeeper came outside for another crate.

"Find some men that can use a rifle," Will shouted, to make himself heard above the screams of the women along the street. "We can pass out some of these new guns and spread men around to protect all sides. If Zambrano finds a weak spot, he'll ride right through it and we're done for."

"I can shoot, and so can John Sikes. Paulito and Juan and Carlos know a rifle. I'll see who I can round up."

Then Ben turned a worried look south. "We'll all be killed, Captain. There's too many of them." He sighed, then was off to find riflemen, dodging wandering women and frightened children milling between the adobes.

Billy caught Will's arm. "I'll take a rifle and plenty of shells to the roof of the cantina, Cap'n. The adobe ledge goes all the way around the top, giving a man cover so he can shoot. This is where they'll hit us, I figure. It's the south edge of town and they can see this wagon plain as day."

Will shook his head, trying to think clearly. "We need shooters covering all sides, somebody who can hit what he aims at. I'll send Carl to the roof of the blacksmith's shop. I'm stayin' on the ground so I can move around and protect a weak flank. Ben Flowers is rounding up a few goatherders who can use a rifle. It won't be much, but it's better'n facing them by ourselves."

Billy fixed Will with a look. "You forgot about the best shooter amongst us, Cap'n. Leon can pick a sand fly off a buzzard's beak at two hundred yards."

"It ain't his fight anymore," Will replied softly. "I wouldn't blame him if he stayed in the cantina and drank whiskey while the rest of us do the fighting."

"He threw in with us once," Billy protested. "He'll do it again, if you ask."

Leon came sweating from the cantina for another box of guns. He looked over at Will and stopped behind the wagon.

"Tell him, Leon," Billy shouted. "Tell him you'll help us fight Zambrano if he gives the order."

Leon blinked, sweat dripping from his chin. "I'd like nothin' better than to kill that dogshit Zambrano, Cap'n. You give the word, and I'll start killin' Mexicans . . . I'll make 'em wish they hadn't come back to Encinal."

A curious light burned behind Leon's eyes, and one corner of his mouth worked into a lopsided grin.

Chapter Fifteen

John Sikes and Arturo worked furiously to unwrap some of the new rifles and clean them with rags. Ben had assembled a ragtag group near the wagon, explaining how the firing mechanisms worked to Paulito and Juan and Carlos and an old man named Delgado. Carl had limped to the north edge of town with two rifles and boxes of shells to take a firing position on the roof of the blacksmith's shop. Billy was on the roof of the cantina now, preparing his weapons, watching the riders advance. Leon disappeared into the stable, helped by a boy who carried a crate of .44/.44 cartridges. Will saw the boy scurry from the stable door. "Señor asks for another rifle," the boy cried, out of breath.

"They're gettin' close, Cap'n," Billy called from the rooftop. "I'd get everybody off the street before the shootin' starts. They'll be in range in a minute or two."

Will wiped the last of the grease from a rifle and gave it to John. "Get someplace where you've got some cover," Will ordered. "And keep your head down."

The blacksmith was off in a lumbering gait toward an adobe hut east of the stable with windows facing the south, his pockets full of paper cartons of shells, the rifle small in his big hands. Ben sent the old man named Delgado to join John. Delgado's head bobbed as he trotted for the hut, cradling his rifle.

Will drew Ben's attention. "Take Paulito and Juan to the well and place them so they can protect the east side of town. Carlos can climb to the roof of your store."

Carlos shook his head. Sweat was pouring down his face as he trotted down the street with a rifle.

"Where's Isabella?" Will asked, before Ben could leave for the well.

"She's rounding up the little children, to hide them inside the church. The walls are thick. Some of the women are helping her."

There was no time to assist Isabella with the children, for now the irregular line of horsemen was very near, and soon the first gunshot would signal an all-out charge toward Encinal. Will saw rifle barrels gleaming in the sunlight. "Maybe most of them are single-shot," he muttered, taking two paper cartons of shells from a crate at the back of the wagon.

Ben ran east with Paulito and Juan, hurrying toward the well. Will then caught a glimpse of Isabella's green dress near the front of the church, herding crying children up the steps. "I guess we're as ready as we're ever gonna be," he said, looking over his shoulder when Carlos appeared briefly on the roof of the dry-goods store. The boy settled behind the adobe ledge and sighted down the barrel of his Winchester. Then Will saw Carl's hat at a corner of the blacksmith's shop.

"I can shoot, señor," someone said behind Will. Arturo had a rifle in his withered hands.

"Get to one of the cantina windows, so you can shoot south," Will explained. "And stay down, old man. There's gonna be a hell of a lot of lead flying this way."

Arturo bowed and hurried inside. The rifles were safely in the cantina, along with the ammunition. Things were set as well as they could be, under the circumstances. Will wondered about the telegraph, and Father Tomas, when suddenly a gun thundered in the distance and Billy cried, "Here they come!"

The rumble of galloping horses sounded from the hills. Will whirled toward the Laredo road. Men were bunching together for the charge to reach the wagon. More were scattered across the hills, churning dust as their horses reached full stride.

He levered a cartridge into the Winchester and tried to guess where the brunt of the attack would fall. Two gunshots popped from the line of charging riders. Someone fired too quickly from the adobe hut beyond the stable, then a woman's scream came from somewhere in the village. Will trotted to one corner of the cantina and brought the Winchester to his shoulder.

He tried in vain to count the horsemen. Moving targets made the task impossible. A puff of smoke came from a distant rifle, and Will heard a bullet whack into the adobe cantina. A gunshot cracked from the trees around the well, then three more in rapid succession. "Wasted shots," Will muttered. "Wait for the range."

Sombreroed horsemen spurred recklessly over uneven ground at full speed, bringing rifles to bear. Here and there they heard the pop of a gunshot. Will's hands made sweat on the rifle stock. He put his sights on a hard-charging sorrel near the front of the attack and lifted the mouth of the Winchester slightly, allowing for the distance. Muscles tightened, he nudged the trigger when he judged the fall of the slug would be right.

The rifle slammed into his shoulder and the explosion made his ears ring. The sorrel swerved when the rider's weight shifted to one side. Slowly, as if in a dream, the rider slid down, his rifle flying from his hands. Arms and legs flailed in a ball of caliche dust. Another rider reined quickly to avoid the fallen man.

Billy's rifle barked and a horse at the front of the pack stumbled. Will grimaced. Horses would die in the hailstorm of bullets—unavoidable at greater range. The rider was pitched face first over the horse's head. A gun thundered from the livery and the Mexican's body jerked before it skittered into the cactus and yucca plants. Leon's gun had been strangely silent—until now. Then guns began to crack all across the village. Will worked the lever and sent a brass shell casing tinkling into the adobe wall beside him. A rivulet of sweat came from his hatband when he tried to find a target; he fingered it away quickly and swung his sights.

BLOODY SUNDAY 135

Pounding hooves distracted him. Four horsemen were bunched for a charge toward the wagon. Will aimed quickly and sought a target among the four. Off to Will's left a gunshot ripped his target from the back of the running horse before he could pull the trigger. Leon's deadly aim sent the rider off the rump of his horse without his sombrero. Will turned his sights and found the chest of a second rider, triggering off a hasty shot that tore the man from his saddle, arms askew, hands clawing empty air.

A gun sounded from the roof of the cantina, then a hollow explosion as Arturo's rifle rang out. A running horse buckled and went down. Another rider swung right to avoid the tumbling animal. Leon fired and the rider flew, arms outstretched like wings before he fell out of sight.

Will levered a shell into the firing chamber and drew a bead on the shape of a man charging through a cloud of dust. His target shifted suddenly and his shot went wide. He readied the gun quickly and heard the sharp report of Leon's rifle. A man was thrown from his speeding mount beneath the heels of onrushing horses. Bullets thudded into the adobe building where Will made his stand. Fragments pattered down on his hat brim. Will clamped his jaw and took aim. The Winchester jolted and his shot missed a charging rider. He cursed his bad luck and sent another shell into the chamber angrily.

Guns were popping near the well, and from the hut beyond the stable. Horses swirled in the corrals, whickering, churning dust. The oncoming riders were very close now—Will could see their bearded faces and hear their angry cries. Billy's rifle banged and a Mexican spun from his saddle into the melee. Will brought his gun muzzle to bear on the closest target and forced himself to take careful aim before he nudged the trigger. A rider slumped over his horse's withers, clutching his leg. His rifle fell. A gun sounded and the rider disappeared.

He could see the galloping horses clearly now, the flaring of nostrils and windblown manes racing toward the cantina. Will thumbed four cartridges into the loading gate as quickly as he could, spilling a part of the handful in his haste when a slug ricocheted into the wall near his face. Before he could swing the rifle to his shoulder, he heard Billy and Leon fire. Two men flung their arms skyward as they left their saddles. Arturo fired from the bowels of the cantina and a wounded man screamed.

Will found the chest of a lone horseman. Crisscrossed bandoleers filled his sights. He squeezed and was rewarded by a heavy kick from the rifle stock. The bandoleers were nowhere in sight. A gunshot echoed from the center of town and Will whirled as he levered another shell. Carlos fired again over the ledge above the store—a cloud of gun smoke swept past his face. The boy moved higher to aim down at a closer target. Will readied a warning shout as Carlos raised himself above the protection of the ledge. Too late, the boy's body jerked as a slug passed through him, spinning him around like a child's top. The rifle flew from his hands before he fell from sight.

"They're coming from the west!" Will cried, breaking into a run. He ran the length of the Agave Cantina and rounded a corner where an alley passed between the cantina and the little bakery where Sanches died. A pair of Mexicans rode hard to make the alley, with pistols barking at the rooftops. Will skidded to a halt and fired his Winchester from the hip. A bearded face mirrored surprise and then sudden pain. Knowing the result, Will jerked the lever as he brought the rifle to his shoulder for a shot at the other rider. The Winchester banged and a sombreroed rider grabbed his chest as he went over the back of his saddle.

Will stumbled headlong down the alley. More men raced their lathered horses through the mesquites behind the cantina, poor targets in the moving limbs until they were very close. Will found the outline of a man hidden behind the pale green leaves. His shot brought a muffled cry from the mesquites, then a riderless horse galloped into the clearing behind the cantina, trailing its reins.

Another horse and rider broke through the tangle of swaying limbs with a pistol aimed at Will. Will crouched and clawed the heavy Walker from his holster. The pistol bucked in his fist as the Mexican's bullet whistled past his cheek. A dozen yards separated the men when the guns exploded, a bay horse at full speed carrying the Mexican closer, laboring under the punishment of spurs. Will's shot brought a crimson splatter to the bare skin below the rider's beard. A strangled cry sounded above the thunder of running hooves, and the man went down heavily on a stretch of hardpan, disjointed limbs bouncing, a hand still gripping the gun.

The bay snorted and swerved, bucking once when its back was free of the rider's weight. A shadow moved in the mesquites and Will swung toward it, dropping to one knee.

Suddenly Carl's shotgun sounded from the blacksmith's shop. A shiver went down Will's spine. "They're closing in now," he whispered, for Zambrano's men were within Betsy's range. Will fired at the shadow with his Walker. Limbs parted and swayed from the passage of speeding lead. Will blinked when the shadow was no longer there. It had been a lucky shot.

A rifle spat flame from the back door of the cantina. The old man had left the window when he heard Will's gunshots. Two muffled explosions came from the mesquite trees behind the cantina, and one bullet made a soft sound, the other a ricochet song.

Arturo staggered from the doorway clutching his stomach, his face twisted with pain. Blood sprinkled from a gaping hole in his back where the slug had passed through his body, making patterns of red where his sandals left their prints in the white dust. The old man walked blindly toward the mesquites where the guns waited, trailing his blood, each faltering step shorter than the other until he finally fell from a booming gunshot.

Will took a wild, angry shot at the puff of gun smoke. His fire was answered quickly by the report of a rifle. Cracking limbs marked the passage of a horse moving through the dense thicket away from the cantina. Will fired again and heard his bullet sing harmlessly high.

A cry came from the other side of town, a piercing scream that set off a volley of gunfire. Will scrambled to his feet and ran through the alley, holstering his Colt, bringing his rifle to bear as he rounded the corner where the wagon sat.

The shrill scream sounded again, a woman's terror from the east side of the village. Guns popped and banged near the well, smoke filtering skyward through tree limbs before the wind swept it away. Carl's rifle thundered from the rooftop, followed by an angry shout. "Missed the sumbitch!" Carl cried, and Will saw Carl moving behind the adobe ledge to a better position, where he fired again.

A bullet plowed dirt near Will's boots. Three horses raced from the south across brush-choked ground, spurred through the spikes and thorns by three Mexican gunmen. A withering blast of rapid gunfire spat from the livery as Leon cut the men down, one by one, until three empty saddles fluttered stirrups in the wind as the horses galloped toward the corrals.

Billy's sweating face appeared above the roof of the cantina. "What happened to the old man?" he cried, thumbing fresh loads into his Winchester.

Will shook his head, aiming a thumb over his shoulder.

Billy understood. He shouldered his rifle and fired, working the muscles in his cheeks before he dropped out of sight below the ledge.

Will ran to the corner of the cantina and searched the dust for a target. Swirls of windblown caliche thickened over the hills to the south. Riderless horses galloped aimlessly back and forth, nickering to each other, moving away from the banging of the guns.

North, Will saw Carl rise above the ledge to take a shot at a bearded man on foot running for the safety of an adobe hut. Carl's bullet struck the man mid-stride; he staggered once, caught himself for another step and then sank to his knees in the dust, one hand reaching for the wound between his shoulder blades. A volley of gunfire near the well drowned out Carl's announcement that the bullet found its mark. The Mexican toppled over and lay still.

Will heard the children screaming inside the church when a brief halt interrupted the gun blasts. Across the village he saw two riderless horses in front of the church. His feet were moving at once through the next volley of whistling lead, for his only thoughts now were of Isabella and the children.

He raced toward the church as hard as he could run, gritting his teeth in savage fury. If any harm came to Isabella or any of the children, he knew he would never forgive himself—the church stood unguarded at the northeast edge of Encinal—it had been his responsibility to assign the building protection, and in the mass of confusion he had forgotten Encinal's greatest treasures, the little ones, and his newfound love who had changed his life so suddenly. His knuckles turned white around his rifle as his boots thumped between adobe dwellings toward the bell he could see above the thatched roofs. "Damn them!" he hissed, sighting the horses and their empty saddles in front of the church when he rounded a corner.

He raced foolishly for the stone steps, tossing his rifle aside to pull his Colt when no one fired at him from the doorway. Guns popped in the distance and he ignored them. It didn't matter now if Zambrano and his men took the rifles. His only thoughts were of Isabella and the *niños* behind the thick adobe walls.

His boot hit the first step and its sound was lost in a chorus of children's screams from inside. Will shouldered into the planking blocking his path and burst into the dark sanctuary amid louder cries when the door flew open.

A stocky Mexican whirled, facing the sunlight spilling into the church from the entrance, a pistol in his fist. Will fired, knowing there were two as his bullet found the first. A piece of cloth vest puffed away from the bullet hole in the man's chest, then blood came squirting from the hole. The roar of the big Walker echoed off the adobe walls like thunder as Will wheeled to find the second gunman in the darkness.

Shrieking children fled in all directions, making Will's task harder with their distraction. The wounded Mexican slumped wetly against the sanctuary wall and slid down to the floor with a thump.

"Will!" a woman's voice cried from across the crowded room. At the altar he saw Isabella's green dress moving through the shadows away from him. He crouched, and a gunshot blasted. A white-hot pain knifed through his left shoulder, spinning him to the floor like the kick of a mule. For an instant he was stunned and could not move. He heard Isabella call out to him again, but now her voice was far away, and the frightened cries of the children seemed less. His shoulder burned and he felt himself slipping toward unconsciousness. Arms trembling, he clamped his jaw and forced his body off the floor, fingers locked around the cold iron of the Walker.

A wave of nausea rendered him weak, yet still he demanded that his muscles obey. He pushed himself to his knees and looked toward the front of the church. A grinning Mexican gunman held Isabella by the arm, jerking her across the floor. A crying child of two or three ran between Will and Isabella, calling Isabella's name, little arms outstretched. The gunman pulled Isabella roughly, then the glint of gun metal took his eyes away from the woman. Will cocked his pistol. The gunman's hand started up with the gun dangling loosely at his side.

The Walker roared and the heavy thump of the .44 slug lifted the Mexican off the floor. His smile twisted, his head thrown back from the force of the bullet shattering his teeth. Isabella screamed. Blood showered over her green dress as the hand gripping her arm relaxed. Booted feet tried in vain to break the fall backward, a dancer's steps to an unheard melody. The body fell heavily on the hard stone floor. The gun clattered beside it, spinning, reflecting sunlight. Last to fall was a dust-caked sombrero, fluttering like a wounded bird, plopping softly on the dead man's chest.

"Oh Will!" Isabella cried, rushing across the floor to kneel at his side. Blood dribbled from a tear in his shirt. He holstered his gun and touched the wound high on his left shoulder. A gash peeled his skin the width of a finger, exposing bloody muscle.

"I'm okay," he whispered, swaying weakly on his knees. "Help me up. I've got to get back and lend the boys a hand."

BLOODY SUNDAY   141

"But you are hurt, Will," she exclaimed. Tears streamed down her soft cheeks. Her beautiful dress was covered with blood.

"They'll kill us all unless we can stop them." He groaned, allowing her to lift him gingerly to his feet by his right arm.

The battle raged beyond the doorway of the church. Guns rattled and men cursed. "Tie something over it to stop the blood," he instructed, "and stay with the children. Can you use a gun?"

She shook her head quickly, removing a green sash from her waist. "I could not shoot, Will. Not even to protect the little ones."

He nodded as she tied the sash in place around his shoulder. "Keep everyone down on the floor, and don't go outside for any reason."

He bent down to pick up his hat, wincing with the effort. He saw blood pooling around the first gunman he shot near the doorway. Heavy-lidded eyes stared blankly at nothing, sightless now.

He ran from the church—each footfall jolted new pain through his damaged shoulder—to the spot where his rifle lay. With the Winchester cradled in his right arm, he swung toward the well, forcing his attention from his wound to the deadly gunblasts around him. The pounding of guns came from all sides. Whistling bullets sped randomly among the adobes, singing their deadly song, spitting dust and adobe fragments as they glanced off buildings and plowed tiny furrows in the caliche.

He found Ben near the well. "Get to the church," Will gasped, out of breath from his run. "I left it unguarded . . . the women and children . . ."

Ben understood. Crouching, he left the trees with a box of shells and a rifle, dodging stray bullets as he hurried away from the well.

Juan was kneeling behind the circle of stones around the well, shooting over the rim when a running horse passed within range. The boy was holding his own. Empty shell casings littered the ground around his feet. Will searched the shadows beneath the trees for Paulito until he found a figure slumped behind a tree trunk.

Will crouched and ran toward the boy. Paulito's face was bathed in sweat and his rifle lay untouched beside him. One quick look told Will why the youth was out of the fight—his right arm was shattered near the elbow. Splinters of bone jutted through his flesh. Blood pooled in the caliche below the tree.

"I cannot shoot, señor," Paulito groaned, his face twisted into a mask of pain. "*Madre* . . . my arm!"

"Lie quiet," Will whispered. "There's nothing anyone can do to help you now."

The boy nodded and closed his eyes. The attack had thinned on the east side of the village and now the gunshots were less.

Will was off at a run for the cantina, wondering if there would be anyone left alive in Encinal when the day was over.

Chapter Sixteen

Carl and Billy were firing less often. Leon's guns were silent. John and Delgado poured bullets out the windows of the adobe at targets too distant for accuracy. From the shaded porch of the cantina Will could see the Mexicans pulling back in widely scattered groups, holding talks when they were out of range on a hilltop. The attackers north of the village slowed their charge. The firing fell to an occasional crack when Carl no longer found targets in front of him.

John and Delgado ceased their firing. Off in the distance Juan's rifle popped once, then an eerie silence spread over Encinal. Wind sighed through the trees behind the cantina. A dog barked, and a wounded horse south of the livery nickered painfully as it tried to hobble away on a shattered foreleg. The smell of gun smoke lessened on the wind.

Someone coughed on the rooftop of Ben's store, and Will remembered Carlos, falling from a bullet. "That kid's hurt," Billy shouted from his perch atop the cantina.

"I'll see what I can do," Will replied, resting his rifle against the cantina wall.

Inside the cantina he found clean rags, and a bottle of tequila to lessen the boy's pain. Glancing over his shoulder, he hurried toward the store, wincing when his gait pained his wound. Near the little telegraph office his boots slowed, for he beheld a sight that twisted his stomach. The old priest lay a few yards from the office door, facedown in a pool of blood, his clean white robe crusted over with dried blood, already swarming with blowflies.

"Damn," Will hissed between clenched teeth, halting near the body. Father Tomas's eyes were open. Green-backed flies moved in and out of his mouth and nose. Will bent over and touched the old man's shoulder. A groan whispered from his chest.

"Somebody lend me a hand!" Will shouted. He rolled the priest over on his back, fighting away flies with the back of his hand. A gaping bullet hole trickled blood down the front of his silky garment. Father Tomas blinked and tried to speak, but the sound was muffled by bloody bubbles from his throat. The bullet had torn a lung, and death was certain now.

Will shaded the priest's face with his hat. "Did you get a message through?" he asked softly.

Heavy boots came running from one of the adobes. John Sikes was ashen as he approached the telegraph office.

Father Tomas wagged his head weakly. No message had gone to San Antonio before the wire went down. Will bit his lip and felt the weight of their plight in Encinal. No soldiers would be coming.

"Help me carry him to the shade," Will said, as John bent down to examine the bullet hole. "He's dying. Let's make him as comfortable as we can."

Sudden tears brimmed in John's eyes. The burly blacksmith wept like a child as they lifted Father Tomas and carried him the few yards to the shade of Ben Flowers's porch. The priest took a gurgling breath when the sun was no longer in his eyes.

"We're all gonna die here today, ain't we?" John asked, peering up at Will when Will started for the back of the store.

Will hesitated and cast a look toward the southern hills. Knots of riders were gathered in the distance, watching Encinal, faces shaded by drooping sombreros. "I reckon that's up to us and how well we shoot these rifles. There ain't no such thing as a fight that can't be won, but this one damn sure has the look of an uphill pull. There's nothing you can do for Father Tomas now. You're needed back at that window. Zambrano and his men will try again."

John shook his head, fingering tears from his tanned cheeks

as he stared down at the priest. "I'll stay just a little while longer, Cap'n Dobbs."

Will found a stack of empty crates against the back wall where Carlos had climbed to the roof. Slowly, painfully, he used his injured shoulder sparingly to reach the top.

Carlos lay on his back on the sod-covered thatchwork roof, his white homespuns now a dirty red. Will crept over the uncertain footing to kneel beside him. The boy had taken a bullet in his left side, just below his armpit. When Will tore his shirt away from the wound, he saw the gleam of white bone protruding from the opening. "Broken rib," Will sighed, with no idea what to do to help the boy. The injury required the skills of a doctor if Carlos's life was to be saved. Will could only hope to stop the bleeding.

Carlos looked at Will, pleading for help with his pain-ridden eyes. "Drink some of this," Will said, offering the tequila. "I can put a piece of rag in the hole, but that's about all I can do for you, son. You fought bravely, Carlos. You made one hell of a soldier."

The boy grinned weakly and swallowed when the bottle touched his lips. *"Gracias, Capitan,"* he croaked when the bitter fluid was swallowed.

Will put the neck of the bottle in Carlos's hand, then he carefully tucked a piece of cloth into the bullet wound. The boy cried out once, arms stiffening, then his face turned hard and he fought the pain in silence.

Will climbed down, scanning the hills, wondering when the next charge would come. He hurried around the corner to the street and heard John Sikes weeping bitterly over the body of Father Tomas. "Come along, John," Will whispered, clapping a hand on the big man's shoulder. "There's nothing you can do here, but there is a town full of women and children who need your steady hands on a rifle."

The big blacksmith came slowly to his feet. Tears streamed down his face. "They didn't have to kill the old priest," he cried. "He didn't have a gun."

Will left him when he saw Carl limping back from the cantina with a bottle in his fist. "Fightin' makes me thirsty."

Carl grinned humorlessly, his sweaty face caked with white dust. "We killed a bunch of the dirty sumbitches, Cap'n. There's dead Meskins layin' all over the place. I blowed one's head plumb off his neck when he rode close enough to use Big Betsy. You oughta seen it, Cap'n. I wish'd you coulda seen it."

Carl was now as crazy as Leon, Will decided, crazed by the nearness of death from all sides. "Get back up on that roof," Will snapped, hurrying off, grinding his teeth to keep more words inside his mouth.

"How's the kid?" Billy asked from his rooftop perch, sipping his own bottle of tequila when Will reached the cantina.

"Busted rib. Lost a lot of blood. They got the old priest, too, and the boy called Paulito has got a broken arm. We were lucky, I guess, that we didn't lose any more."

"How bad's the shoulder?" Billy asked.

"A scratch. Went clean through. Hurts like hell, but I'll live."

Billy hoisted his bottle. "This agave squeeze makes a mighty good remedy for whatever ails you. Steadies the nerves to boot. Are the women and kids okay at the church?"

Will shook his head, remembering the close brush with death inside the sanctuary. "Ben Flowers is there now. Him and Juan are all that's left on the east side. Maybe I oughta send ol' Delgado over. . . ."

Billy squinted into the heat haze. "They're gatherin' just now, Cap'n. Something's afoot. Whatever you aim to do, you'd best get it done in a hurry. Looks like they're gettin' ready for another charge."

Groups of horsemen trotted together near the fence around the Encinal cemetery. Dust boiled skyward from the moving horses. Will watched the men assemble in a loose-knit circle around a big Mexican on a prancing black horse. "That'll be Zambrano in the middle," Will declared. "I saw one of 'em keeping off to himself while the rest did the fighting, and I reckon that was him. Smart son of a bitch—lettin' the others test our defenses."

BLOODY SUNDAY   147

"Maybe he ain't nothin' but a coward," Billy suggested. "He lets his men do the dying."

Will didn't waste words giving an answer, starting for the adobe where Delgado fought alongside John. Leon and Billy and he could defend the south side of town, and the west if the tide turned, so Carl could add to the cross-fire. Their weak flank was the east side of town, and if Zambrano was a capable leader, he would sense it.

The old man sat patiently near a window. Two rifles rested on the floor near his feet. Spent cartridges lay all over the room, a room still smelling of burning gunpowder and sweat. John sat beside another window with his rifle cradled in his lap. His tears for the dead priest had dried, but his eyes were still red-rimmed, watery.

"Delgado, take your guns to the well where Juan is fighting. The boy, Paulito, is hurt. Take a bottle of tequila to the boy. It's about all we can do for him now."

The old man shook his head and gathered his rifles and boxes of ammunition. He paused near the door and looked over his shoulder at Will. "Maybeso their *caballos* need water soon, *Capitan*. A horse don't run so good when it is thirsty."

Delgado's sandals crunched away from the adobe. Will looked out the window, thinking how right Delgado was about the horses. The animals would need water, and Zambrano would have to make a choice. The well in Encinal was the only water north of the border for many miles. Water-starved horses wouldn't make much of a charge.

"We need to guard that well," John offered. "Maybe I oughta go with Delgado?"

"Not just yet," Will sighed, guessing how things would go. "They'll try for the rifles first. If we keep them pushed back, then they'll have no choice but to fight us for the well, to keep their horses alive."

Will judged the time. The sun had moved overhead, and now it baked the dry prairie with all its fury. The heat and the wind would be on the side of Encinal.

On the walk back to the cantina he tried to count the men

assembled around Zambrano. Loose horses still wandered the brush nibbling sparse grass, empty saddles gleaming in the sun. Better than thirty mounted men listened to Zambrano's instructions beside the cemetery, rifle barrels poised, awaiting orders. "If they come together in one rush, some of them will make it through and we'll have them all around us." Wondering aloud, he decided to call Carl down from the rooftop. Every gun would be needed to face the brunt of the attack.

He hurried to the blacksmith's shop. "Get down, Carl. I figure they'll make a charge straight for the wagon. It's a gamble, but one we'll have to take. If a few of them circle around to try us from the north, we can skirt the road and hurry back this way."

Carl grunted and took a huge swallow of tequila before he started down.

They came toward Encinal slowly, bunched together as Will figured all along, headed for the cantina. Trotting horses made dust above the Laredo road.

"Here the bastards come," Carl announced needlessly. Every eye was trained on the advancing army of gunmen. Drooping sombreros shaded the faces of the riders. Guns glinted in the blinding sunlight.

"Zambrano's with 'em this time," Billy observed softly.

At the front of the trotting horses was a lathered black mount, prancing under a tight rein. Its rider sat erect, face unwaveringly upon the wagon in front of the cantina. A rifle butt rested on the rider's knee, barrel toward the sun. Still out of range, Zambrano rode proudly at the head of his mounted men.

Suddenly the horses were moving, spurred to a lope under a swirling cloud of dust. Riders at the rear spread outward, riding faster to reach the front of the charge. Hooves thundered over the caliche hardpan, rumbling like distant drums. It was a sight that would strike fear into the hearts of brave men, Will knew, as he watched the ominous cloud of dust roll across the prairie on a westerly wind. He wondered if Leon or Carl now felt the slightest twinges of fear.

Shouts echoed from the road. The first gunshot popped and a bullet whined into the cantina wall. Big John Sikes started shooting from his window, but no Ranger fired, awaiting the right range.

Absently, Will noticed that Zambrano was no longer at the front. Charging horses made it impossible to find him in the mass of flying manes and tails. "Smart bastard," Will whispered, sighting down his Winchester.

Leon found the range first. His gun exploded and a rider went down. Angry yells came from the advancing army, and guns banged an answer to Leon's first shot. Carl and Billy started shooting and the sound of booming rifles filled Will's ears. Will found a target and let the hammer fall. The rifle bucked in his hands and a Mexican reeled from his saddle, tossing his gun in the air as he fell.

Leon's Winchester laid down a murderous volley of gunfire. Horses stumbled and riders fell as if the animals had run across gopher holes. A falling horse screamed. Above the din Will heard the sickening snap of a foreleg. Billy poured bullets into the charge from the rooftop. Two men dropped from their horses and Carl shouted a whoop of delight.

Will fired and missed, then fired again. Shots banged from John's window. Leon suddenly opened up with a newly-loaded gun and more horses went down, tails and manes floating when the animals halted so quickly. Withering gunfire erupted from Carl's position at a cantina window. Wounded men cried and caught their chests, rolling from saddles into the churning dust.

The charge was broken as quickly as it was begun. Riders split away and spurred to either side, bent low over their saddles to dodge flying lead. Crippled horses and wounded men floundered across the wagon ruts, veiled by dust clouds, moving away from unending volleys of deadly bullets from Encinal. Carl whooped and yelled, cursing the Mexicans, still pumping bullets at any moving target. Leon fired less often now, but each time with unerring result.

From the corner of his eye Will saw three horsemen charge the well. Rifles popped for the first time at the eastern edge of the village. Will broke into a run toward the trees where Juan and Delgado put up their valiant fight. One rider spilled from his saddle near the goat pens, bouncing on his back, skidding over the caliche until a clump of cactus halted his slide. Two more raced past Juan and Delgado, spurring as they fired pistols over their shoulders. They were between the adobe huts quickly, out of the line of fire from the trees. Will stumbled to a halt and raised his rifle; a moving target appeared in his sights, and he feathered the trigger as the horses galloped down on him.

A bandoleered chest exploded in a shower of blood and leather. The buckskin horse shied and the body aboard its back swayed. Will hurriedly levered the Winchester and swung his sights. A muzzle flashed atop the back of a galloping bay running neck and neck with the buckskin. Will felt something pop against his forehead and his vision dimmed.

He knew he was falling, and he was powerless to help himself as blue sky appeared before his eyes. His head slammed against the ground. A black fog enveloped him like a blanket. Flashing points of light surrounded him. He heard horses galloping past him, and then the earth shuddered beneath him when a clap of thunder shook the skies above Encinal.

His last conscious thought was one of wonder, how it could rain from cloudless blue skies. He listened again for the thunder, waiting for raindrops to pelt his face, when slowly his body lifted and he was carried off into a silent black mist.

Chapter Seventeen

Hazy shapes flickered, then disappeared. Muffled voices came and went, saying things he could not understand. The world around him was black . . . total darkness like the dark at the back of the secret cave above the Bosque where he hid from his father when he was a small boy, ducking his chores.

A point of light appeared and the darkness grayed. A voice spoke to him, talking gibberish. He tried to answer the voice, yet his reply was nonsense, nothing but tangled words and meaningless sounds.

Something cool touched his face. Slowly his vision cleared. A face hovered above him and he tried to focus. His surroundings danced before his eyes when a wave of dizziness swept him away from the light. His senses told him he was moving, though he made no effort to do so on his own. The black fog returned. He cried out, fearing the fog, not wanting to be alone, but his cry echoed hollowly and he gave himself up to the dark.

A stab of pain awakened him. He blinked and tried to get his bearings. Someone spoke to him . . . he recognized his name and tried desperately to see his surroundings clearly. A face took shape before his eyes, a woman's face. The woman smiled, and her smile was so beautiful that he thought this must be some wonderful dream. Blinking, he tried to sit up and quickly felt the pressure of a hand against his chest.

"Lie still," the beautiful woman scolded. He knew her voice then . . . recognized its soft inflection, yet he could not remember her name, try as he might.

"Where am I?" he whispered, his voice sounding distant, like an echo from a canyon's walls.

"In the cantina. Now lie still while I put a bandage around your head."

"My head? What happened to me?" His words croaked from his throat, a bullfrog's sound. He wondered why he was in a cantina, searching his memory for a recollection, his mind still blank.

"A bullet creased your forehead, Will. You lost a lot of blood."

A sudden flash of memory returned—the guns booming all around him. He was in Encinal, and they were in a fight for their lives. "I remember now. Help me up and find my rifle."

He tried to sit again and the woman's hand halted him. Her name was Isabella, he knew now, and she was the most beautiful woman he ever met.

"You must rest first," she insisted, "while I put beef tallow on your wounds so the blood will stop."

He relaxed and listened for the sound of guns. "What about Zambrano?" he asked, thinking how feeble his words seemed, barely rising from his chest. He heard only silence. What had happened to the bang of the guns?

"Zambrano has pulled back. The Ranger named Carl said they lost too many men when they came a second time."

He remembered the second charge . . . falling men and horses tumbling to the ground in a hail of bullets . . . the three men who charged the well, one downed by Delgado's rifle and a second by Will's hurried shot. The third rider had fired point-blank in Will's face before he could get off a shot. He remembered his fall. Everything was coming back to him.

Isabella wound a strip of cloth around his head. "There," she said, finished. "This will have to do for now."

"Help me up," he said, pushing an elbow back to lift his weight from the prone position. Pain reminded him of his injured shoulder, making him hesitate until Isabella took his right arm.

Cold sweat beaded his face. He discovered himself on the floor of the cantina, seated on a blanket. A lantern burned on a nearby table. With Isabella's help he climbed unsteadily to his feet. Trembling knees threatened to buckle under his weight and a dizzy sickness washed through his skull. He righted himself against a table and took a deep breath.

"You must rest," Isabella warned, gripping his right arm to steady him.

"Help me outside first. I've got to see that my men are okay, and the others."

Reeling against Isabella on weakened legs, he hobbled to the door and felt the wind on his face, drying the clammy sweat. On the porch he frowned, noticing a late evening sky overhead.

"How long was I out cold?" he asked, stepping gingerly to a wheel of the freight wagon where he could balance himself.

"Four or five hours," she replied darkly, searching his face when he gritted his teeth to stay upright. "You must rest, Will. There was so much blood. . . ."

He saw Carl and Leon near the stable. Beyond the outskirts of Encinal the hills were empty. He wondered where Zambrano had gone, and if the battle were truly over. "Get me a bottle of tequila . . . and my rifle."

She scowled, then turned obediently and hurried inside the cantina in her ruined green dress. Will gripped the wagon wheel and took stock of his surroundings.

Bodies lay in the street, and he sought to identify them with a silent wish that none would be men from Encinal. A bearded pistolero lay on his back beside the stable, chalky with dust, swarming with blowflies. Beyond the cantina on the Laredo road the brushland was littered with corpses, those of horses and men. Buzzards circled and perched atop the carrion, hopping from one feeding place to the next. A red sunset bathed the pale prairie with its blood colors, a fitting hue for the grisly battlefield around Encinal. The fight to claim the wagonload of rifles had become a war. When the lost lives were counted, the story would fill newspaper headlines across the state . . . perhaps across the entire country. The conflict would have far-reaching effect on relations with Mexico. Gazing across the battle scene, Will hoped it was ended. A few brave men had turned the tide of battle against overwhelming odds.

He heard footsteps and swung a glance toward the sound. Billy came down the street from the north end of town, balancing a rifle in his fist. He saw Will and grinned.

"You look sicker'n a foundered mule, Cap'n, but I'm glad to see you made it through."

Will shook his head and regretted it at once, for the movement pained his skull anew. "Tell me what happened. Isabella says I was out cold for several hours."

Billy looked at the prairie and swept a hand south. "They withdrew yonder-ways after they had themselves a parley at the cemetery. Ain't many left, Cap'n—maybe a dozen or so. If I had to take a guess, I'd say they won't be back. Single-shot rifles and pistols don't stack up against these repeaters from the back of a horse. Leon went out a little while ago and took a count. Said there was twenty-nine dead Mexicans out there . . . some of 'em wasn't dead until Leon finished 'em off, so they wouldn't come crawlin' into town when it got dark."

Isabella appeared with tequila. Will took it and gave her a grin before uncorking the jug. "Thanks . . . this'll make medicine for the pounding between my ears."

She returned his smile. "I must go, to help with the others at the church," she said, her smile fading. "My father found a bottle of laudanum at the store. Poor Carlos and Paulito are in such terrible pain."

"We got the wounded boy off the roof, Cap'n," Billy said. "Old Delgado took a bullet above his knee, and the boy with the busted arm looks mighty bad, but I reckon he'll live. Carlos needs a doctor. If we knew the way south was clear, we could hitch up this wagon and haul the wounded to Laredo."

"It could be risky," Will replied, sipping tequila as Isabella hurried toward the church. The sharp bite of the tequila helped to clear his head. He took another swallow. "Safest thing is to wait till morning. Just now I'm not thinkin' straight enough to decide."

Billy took the bottle Will offered. "You had a close call when that bullet grazed your head. You're lucky you ain't got a hole in your skullbone. That pistolero swung around and he was fixin' to finish the job when Carl cut him in half with ol' Betsy. Made a hell of a mess. Leon ran out of the livery and carried you to the cantina before the rest of them got past us. I figure he saved your skin, him and Carl."

"I owe them," Will agreed, watching Carl tilt back a bottle of tequila near the corrals. "You men fought as hard as any men who ever wore a Ranger's star. You're due a commendation from the major."

Billy had something on his mind. He took another sip from the jug. "The way I see it, Cap'n, that oughta include Leon. He put his life on the line to help the rest of us. I say he's earned the right to wear his badge."

Will found himself torn again by emotions—the right and the wrong of things. A part of him argued that Leon deserved a second chance as a Texas Ranger, proving his courage the way he had to protect the rifles. And there was a personal debt to be paid, for Leon risking his hide to carry him to the cantina when the gunfight was at its worst. Still, there was a lingering sense of the way fairness should be handled. Leon had disobeyed the law that a Ranger stood for. How could Will turn his back on it and call it fair to the other Rangers?

Will sighed. "I reckon I'll have to think things through."

John Sikes rounded a corner, walking slowly toward the end of the street, a downcast look on his face. Dried blood was smeared down his shirtfront and trousers. Will wondered if the old man had been hit in the fracas.

"I carried Father Tomas to his hut," John said sadly, a tear glistening in each eye. "He was light as a feather . . . didn't hardly weigh nothin' at all. The children started crying when they saw him. They loved him, and so did I."

"He died trying to help us save the children," Will said quietly. "The bartender, Arturo, gave his life for the people of Encinal. The boy named Carlos may not live through the night, and Paulito has a shattered arm. There may be others. Everyone fought bravely to defend the town."

John shook his head. "It just don't seem right that the priest had to die." He looked toward the south. "I hope it's over now. We've got some more buryin' to do."

John shuffled off, hands in his pockets. Will waited until he was out of earshot. "As soon as it gets dark I want you and Carl back on those roofs. Zambrano and his men might make another try after the sun goes down."

Billy squinted at the horizon. "I never figured he'd come back the first time. I'll hand that Mexican one thing—he's a determined son of a bitch."

Cool night breezes lessened the blood smell from the hills, and the vultures departed with the coming of dark. Lanterns burned behind the village windows. For the first time since early morning, Encinal seemed at peace.

Will walked beside Isabella away from the church. The boy, Carlos, rested in a fevered sleep on a pile of blankets near the altar. Paulito groaned and dozed fitfully, his arm splinted by Ben Flowers, his belly full of laudanum. Delgado hobbled past Will and Isabella on a makeshift crutch, hurrying home to his wife when the goats were fed in the pens.

"You feel better?" Isabella asked, watching his face.

"Near good as new. My head hurts some."

"Are you hungry? I am going home to fix my father something to eat."

"No thanks. I've got to take a turn at the watch. My men haven't had any sleep. I'm not really hungry. Will you stay at the church with your father?"

"Of course. He needs my help with the wounded."

Will halted and looked down at her. "Then I'll say good night. If you need anything, I'll be at the cantina."

She stood on her toes and kissed him, but her face was filled with sorrow. "It was so sad . . . about Father Tomas, and Arturo. I will pray that this terrible trouble is over for us."

She hurried away in her bloodstained dress. He watched her go, until she was out of sight behind an adobe. He knew then just how much he loved her. The battle at Encinal was enough to convince him that his Rangering days were at an end. The choice seemed simple enough now, a twenty-five-dollar-a-month job dodging bullets weighed against a life shared with Isabella. His choice was already made. Turning in his badge was simply a formality.

He approached the cantina and saw Carl's face and shoulders above the ledge around the roof. "All's quiet, Cap'n," Carl announced. "There's some coyotes out there chewin' on the bones the buzzards left 'em. You feelin' okay?"

Will swept the silent hills carefully without answering. He saw a silver-bellied coyote trot across a stretch of barren ground, sniffing the carcasses, pausing to feed. "Keep a sharp eye on things, Carl. If I was in Zambrano's boots, I'd slip back when it got dark and try coming in on foot. Maybe it's over, but I ain't gonna breathe easy until we've got those rifles to San Antone."

"He'd be a fool, Cap'n. I say he's tucked tail and run."

"You were wrong before. Stay awake up there and give a yell if you see anything you don't recognize. I'll take a rifle over to the well and watch the east side."

Carl shook his head. "Billy's on the roof of the blacksmith's shop. Leon, he said he was gonna nose around a little. Never saw which way he went."

Will was puzzled by Leon's disappearance. "You reckon he's out there in the hills?"

"Hard to say, Cap'n. Ol' Leon's brain don't work the same as most others. He's liable to turn up most anyplace. I wouldn't let him worry me none. Leon can take care of himself."

Will entered the empty cantina and found his rifle and hat on a tabletop beside his duster. He left the coat because of his sore shoulder, taking a bottle of tequila after he placed his hat lightly on his head. Pocketing a handful of shells, he walked out to the silent street and looked both ways. The prairie was empty, bathed in soft starlight.

He trudged past the livery and lamplit adobes to the trees surrounding the well. A coyote's sudden bark stiffened his hands around the rifle stock briefly. "Jumpy, ain't you?" he asked himself.

Chapter Eighteen

His eyes were playing tricks on him. Shadows moved and became the outlines of men crouching in the brush, then the shadows would dissolve magically to nothing. Once, a coyote trotted to a hilltop and halted to scent the wind, looking over its shoulder at Will's hiding place beneath the trees. Off in the distance the coyote's mate barked. The animal quickly disappeared into the yucca spikes.

A desert owl hooted. The sound sent a shiver down Will's back. Later, a kid goat bleated. Beads of sweat formed on Will's face and neck, trickling down his spine, plastering his shirt to his skin. He was on edge without apparent reason. The prairie around the village was peaceful, quiet, as it should be. He wondered why his nerves were raw.

Coppery blood smell came on the wind, evoking recollections of the pitched battle. Before noon tomorrow the sun would bloat the corpses, making the grisly burials worse for the men who drew the chore. The battlefield littered with bodies brought back dark memories of the war . . . scenes he had tried to forget in the years since. Fighting Indians seemed different somehow; they were less human in some indefinable way, unlike the men he fought and killed in blue uniforms, often mere boys not unlike himself, fitted in baggy pants and coats two sizes too large, dead from a rifle ball before they were old enough to shave. Thinking about the men he killed in his lifetime, he knew with absolute certainty that he was ready to give it up. What years he had left he meant to live in peace with Isabella. Men like Carl and Billy and Leon could fight the battles to preserve law and order without the help of William Lee Dobbs. He'd done his share. Today's fight had been enough to convince him that he was finished with guns and killing. This particular bloody Sunday reminded him of his age. Twice, he'd been a fraction too slow. Only a fool would think his luck would last forever.

He swallowed more tequila and stared at the brush, thinking of Isabella now. A beautiful young woman awaited his proposal of marriage, and he vowed not to keep her waiting much longer. When the rifles reached San Antonio, he would be free to do whatever he wanted, and what he wanted most was to feel Isabella's soft skin against his and hear her whispered promises of the happiness they would share. She was the most beautiful woman he had ever seen, and she was his for the asking. And ask he would, when he came back to Encinal.

Glancing at the well, he remembered the feel of her body in his arms and the velvet softness of her lips. A grin creased his face as he lost himself in the memory.

The tequila dulled his senses, an explanation for the nearness of the footsteps before he awakened to the sound. He spun around with the rifle and saw a black-suited figure approaching the well.

"It's me," Ben Flowers said quietly, carrying a rifle loosely in one hand. "I thought I heard something near the church, so I came out to have a look around."

Will relaxed. "Haven't seen a thing over here . . . a few coyotes now and then. What was it you heard?"

Ben halted in the deeper shadows below the limbs and scratched his chin. "Hard to say. A voice, maybe."

Will scanned the hills east of town. The brushland seemed empty. "I reckon we're all a little edgy after the fight."

Ben mopped his brow with a handkerchief. "Carlos is in bad shape. He needs a doctor. Tomorrow morning we'll put him in one of the donkey carts piled with straw, so the bumps won't jar his ribs any worse than necessary. I hope he can survive the ride to Laredo. Surely by tomorrow we'll know the bandits are gone."

BLOODY SUNDAY

Will nodded. "Delgado was right—they'll have to find water for their horses. I figure they're at the river by now."

Ben's shoulders sagged. "This has been the bloodiest day in the history of Encinal, Captain. Since Sheriff Wheeler died, there has been a river of blood running through our town, and there's no logical explanation for it. This is a quiet village where simple people tend their goats. Why has all this blood been spilled here?"

"No answer makes any sense," Will sighed. "This town had the misfortune of being a meeting place for the *bandidos* and a wagon full of guns. Bein' close to the border, I reckon. It was just a piece of bad luck."

Ben folded his handkerchief and tucked it away in his pocket. "So many bodies . . . the smell of death is everywhere. I can't think about it. I wonder if I'll ever be able to sleep. I'm afraid to close my eyes. . . ."

Will offered the tequila silently. Ben waved it away with a hand. "Time will soften the memory of it," Will said. "You have to wash the blood off your hands and go on with your lives. It won't be easy."

Ben shouldered his rifle and turned for the church. "I'd better go back. Looks like I was hearing things. Good night, Captain."

He started away from the trees, entering patches of starlit ground where no shadows fell. Will leaned against a tree trunk and tilted back the bottle. Stinging tequila bubbled down his throat, watering his eyes. Ben clumped past the goat pens. Hungry goats begged him for food from the darkness. Will corked the bottle and placed it beside the tree.

A gunshot thundered. Will tensed and shoved away from the mesquite. Ben crumpled to the ground, groaning, his rifle clattering beside him. Will was running toward him before the echo of the shot faded.

Moving shadows, men on foot, bobbed and darted from the brush behind the church. A gun spat flame, then a bullet whined into the tree limbs behind Will. Crouching, he dodged back and forth to make a difficult target. Off in the distance he heard Carl's angry shout.

A silhouette trotted along the pale wall of the church with a gun aimed in front of him. Will whipped the rifle to his shoulder and fired on the run, blinking when his muzzle flash blinded him briefly. The running man slammed into the adobe and triggered his gun wildly as he fell.

Two shots banged from the darkness. Will whirled and sent a bullet toward the flashes of bright light. Levering a shell, he heard a slug whistle overhead, knifing through the wind.

"Goddamn Meskins all over the place!" Carl cried, rattling his spurs in Will's direction. A sudden chorus of bleating goats drowned out the rustle of dry brush and the thump of running feet when more shadows ran toward the back of the church.

Will dropped his rifle and ran forward in a crouch with his pistol. Darting shadows made impossible shots against a night sky. Out in the open Will was making another fool's move, yet his thoughts were of Isabella—he had to reach the front of the church before Zambrano's men.

A gun banged and a piece of lead freckled his face with its dust when the shot fell short. Weaving, he made for the shadow of a burro cart. His head began to swim from the sudden exertion; he stumbled and fell flat, skidding on his chest. Sides heaving, he blinked the dust from his eyes and aimed.

A square of light appeared on the stone steps leading to the church, and in its brilliance he saw a woman step through the door framed by lantern glow. "No!" he cried, his heart in his throat. "Get back!"

Booted feet scurried near the goat pens. He glimpsed a man's head and shoulders, hunkered down, running toward the church. Will swung the Walker and steadied his hand. Behind him he heard Carl clomping closer, gasping for air, the irregular gait of his limp identifying the Ranger.

Will squeezed off a shot and heard the thump of his bullet against something soft. A shuddering cry came from the goat pens and then a body fell. Suddenly guns fired in unison from the dark and he was surrounded by whistling lead. He had marked his position with his muzzle flash and now every gun was trained on him, spitting bullets, spewing dirt near his face. He rolled to shield his body behind the wheel of the cart. A slug splintered the wheel and plopped softly in the dust.

A roar blocked out every other sound, ringing through the village, echoing off the adobes. Molten shot splattered through the mesquite brush and cholla, shredding everything in its path. Voices cried out, men cursing, others yelling, stung by the shot from Carl's shotgun at long range. Carl's spurs advanced again. Shadows moved through the brush as Will struggled to his feet.

"Behind the church, Carl!" Will shouted. A figure started away from one corner of the building. Will aimed too quickly and his bullet skittered off the adobe, whining. Will ducked and raced across the open ground to the spot where Ben lay motionless on his belly.

He seized Ben's coat collar and strained to pull him toward the church, scrambling for purchase with his boot heels. A gun exploded and the shot whispered near, caressing Will's cheek with its hot breath. Ten yards more and Will made the steps, gasping for air, his head reeling with dizzy sickness. A tremendous pull lifted Ben to the entrance. Isabella was crouching near the door, hands to her face. When she saw her father, she screamed.

Will collapsed on the floor, out of breath, losing consciousness. Weak from blood loss, his muscles refused his commands. He forced his eyelids open and drew an arm under him. Isabella knelt over her father's body, tears spilling down her face.

"Stay down," Will gasped. "Get away from the door."

She did not hear him, for her shoulders shook with sobs and a wail of anguish escaped the hand pressed over her mouth. He summoned his strength and got his feet planted, then he stood up and pulled Ben's body against the wall.

Guns exploded outside, the lighter chatter of pistols and the thud of rifles. Off in the distance, behind the church, he heard galloping horses. The hoofbeats grew louder.

Panting, leaning against the wall, he thumbed open the loading gate and ejected spent shells from his Colt. He fingered .44's from the cartridge loops of his gun belt and quickly loaded the gun, his heart breaking for Isabella when he heard her crying.

"Don't come out for anything," he snapped, then he was around the door frame on trembling legs, searching for a target amid the popping of guns.

A rifle spat deadly fire from the trees around the well, shooting into the brush. It was friendly fire. Will tried to find Carl and saw no one among the adobes. Behind the church the rattle of horseshoes was very close now. Will stumbled off the steps and fell against the corner of the building, waiting for the horses with his gun poised in a clammy fist.

Spurs clanked against a horse's ribs, and Will could almost reach out and touch the nearness of the animal. Will's jaw clamped and he swung around the corner, aiming high.

Two running horses raced along the wall of the church. One rider cast a curious shadow, different somehow, his hat brim blown high off his forehead. Will fired for the rider's chest, then swung his gunsights to the other and triggered again.

One man cried and slipped sideways from his saddle. The riderless horse bounded past. The second horseman reined his mount sharply around the corner. A lathered black gelding slid to a halt in the square of lantern light from the church doorway. Will saw the rider's face as the barrel-chested Mexican aimed a plated pistol; the big sombrero did not hide the jagged blue scar down the Mexican's cheek. Time was frozen for the instant their eyes met—this was Zambrano, and Will's chance to end things between them.

Both guns fired at once. Will's left leg cracked and gave way. There was no pain, only the sensation of falling as he fell away from the corner of the church without the use of his leg.

Zambrano's horse reared. The bearded face turned attention to the animal when Will collapsed on his side. Will knew he could not have missed, and yet he had . . . somehow. The

Walker came up as if by sheer will of its own and thundered in Will's hand.

Zambrano's eyes widened, cast down at Will. The black horse shied from the gunshot and Zambrano swayed . . . his hands reached for the saddle horn . . . his pistol fell. The black beard parted in an angry snarl, then his hands missed the saddle horn and Zambrano toppled heavily to the church steps. He groaned, stirring, working his hands to right himself.

Something gripped Will that was beyond his control, a savage thing, overpowering the inner voice that told him Zambrano was out of the fight. Something inside Will demanded vengeance, a force that brought him trembling to his hands and knees, crawling across the hardpan toward Zambrano, mindless of the broken bone grinding inside his left thigh. He reached the steps, sweat beading on his face, shaking violently with exertion and rage. He crawled to Zambrano's chest and stared down at the twisted purple scar.

"You're a hard bastard to kill, Emelio," Will hissed as he stuck the barrel of his Walker in the bandit's mouth. "This is for the little boy . . . and Ben Flowers . . . and the old priest!"

His finger curled and the church steps turned crimson.

Chapter Nineteen

He sat on the veranda sipping good Kentucky whiskey, idly watching the river at sunset from his hotel room. Sluggish current carried bits of driftwood and other flotsam toward the distant Gulf beneath purpling pink skies reflected off the river's smooth surface. His crutches lay across a chair beside him, requirements for his mobility. The leg was better now. In a week or two he would be able to ride.

The ride north would be a bittersweet affair. The pain in his leg would seem small beside the ache in his chest when he rode wide of Encinal on his way home. It was pointless to argue with Isabella over it—she had her duty to perform, not unlike his, though for very different reasons. Her father required continual care, and Doc Warren had said it would always be thus, with the bullet lodged against his spine. Ben Flowers would be a cripple until he drew his last breath, and Will knew his faithful daughter would be beside him until then, running the dusty little store in a forgotten corner of South Texas desert.

Her memory demanded that he drink more whiskey, to soften the recollections of her soft skin and chocolate eyes. For weeks now he had tried to drink himself past the pain of it, without result. As the days stretched into weeks, his longing for Isabella only grew stronger, haunting his sleep, filling his days with emptiness. He wondered if he would ever close his eyes without seeing her beautiful smile, pained by the certainty that she would never be his wife, as in the foolish dreams he dreamed before the final battle at Encinal.

He remembered the morning he was loaded into the burro

cart, wracked by blinding pain when the slightest movement jostled his leg. Beside him lay Ben Flowers, half conscious on a blood-soaked blanket, and on the other side was Carlos, eyes glazed, unaware of his surroundings, near death. Paulito rested against the sides, shoulders tented to carry his broken arm. The ambulance cart made a slow, bumpy journey to Laredo seeking Doc Warren with the handful of wounded soldiers who had defended the village, escorted by two mounted goatherders with new Winchester rifles. And beside the cart rode Isabella on Will's rangy dun, ministering to the injured during their frequent stops. Will remembered only bits and pieces of the trip, fighting the pain between lapses into fevered sleep.

He'd sent the wagonload of guns north with Carl and Billy and Leon, hoping to forever rid himself of the lure of so much firepower within a day's ride of weapon-hungry revolutionaries below the river. Some of Zambrano's men had escaped toward the border. Word of the Winchesters would spread across the mountains of northern Mexico. Will sent instructions that a platoon of cavalry was needed to patrol the river until things quieted down. Enough blood had been shed at Encinal over contraband guns. It was up to the army to see that the border was safe from more invasions.

Before they helped him into the cart, he had given Leon his badge, to put the business to rest over his reinstatement. The incident would be overlooked when Ranger headquarters wired Mexico City about Colonel Diaz's involvement in gun smuggling to a band of revolutionaries. Diaz would vanish, ending any official protest over Leon's ride to Nuevo Laredo. A dark corner of Will's brain still held arguments that Leon Graves was poorly suited to be a peace officer, yet in a stretch of country where lawless men used a slender ribbon of river to flaunt the law, he supposed Leon was no worse than the men he was being paid to control. Deadly force was the only thing some men understood, and if Ranger Leon Graves was nothing else, he was a deadly adversary. As was Carl Tumlinson. The best that could be said about Billy Blue was that he was only slightly more refined. In dangerous country they were good men to side with—Will never questioned their courage. If a man was trying to bring law and order to the Texas border, he couldn't pick three men any better to handle the task.

In the weeks since Isabella's return to Encinal with her father, he'd had lots of time to think about his future. Their parting had been a somber affair—she had cried against his chest as the words spilled out, about duty and love for her father, things he understood, though his heart was breaking. Their short love affair ended when a bullet robbed Ben Flowers of the use of his legs, and Will knew Isabella could make no other choice. He said nothing that would make her decision more difficult. He held her in his arms and told her that he understood, then he kissed her and watched her ride toward Encinal in the burro cart, thus ending his dreams of a quiet life with a woman he could love. He decided then, as he watched the cart roll out of sight over a hill, that for some men a peaceful existence simply wasn't in the cards. He supposed he had cast his lot when he joined the Confederate Army at seventeen. Since, using a gun had become second nature. He killed without remorse now, and once, with his gun in Zambrano's mouth, he actually took pleasure in killing. He wondered if he was now no different than Leon— finding satisfaction in it.

Will drained his glass and stared at the river, knowing his die was cast. He would ride with the Rangers until a bullet took him down, for he knew nothing else. And he was good at the job. Rangering really wasn't so bad, he told himself. A man got used to the loneliness after a while, and there was a certain amount of pride attached to it when the job was done right. Somehow, he would forget Isabella. Somehow.

A tap on the door awakened him from his thoughts. "It's open," he muttered, his voice thickened by whiskey.

Travis Hollaman pushed the door aside. He saw Will on the veranda and clumped across the floor to the opening. "You tryin' to drown yourself with that stuff?" Travis asked, eyeing the jug on the table beside Will.

"I reckon," Will sighed, turning back to the river again.

"It's that woman, ain't it?"

Will nodded. "Can't seem to get her off my mind, Trav. I damn sure tried."

Travis pulled up a chair and fisted the whiskey. A swallow bubbled down his throat in the silence. "Never had you figured for the type to go loco over a woman, Will."

Will shrugged, "Never happen before, not till now."

"It'll pass," Travis said quietly. "Give it time."

Will took the bottle and poured. "Right now I ain't so sure, seein' as I've tried to drink Laredo dry and it seems worse'n ever. This damn leg don't help matters much. I'm stuck on those crutches for another week, the doc says."

"There's some good news," Travis replied. "Got a wire from San Antonio. The army has the rifles, and Hickok is in jail."

Will chuckled, remembering Hickok the morning after the final gunfight. Nicked in the shoulder and without his horse, Leon found him wandering in the brush. It was Hickok who had ridden past the church alongside Zambrano. Will's hasty shot had knocked him from his saddle, out cold. Leon brought him back to town at gunpoint, then he fastened a lariat around Hickok's neck and made him march toward San Antonio in the freight wagon's dust with his hands manacled behind his back. Hickok looked unhappy over the arrangement, never realizing just how lucky he was that Leon let him live to make the walk away from Encinal.

"It's over, then," Will sighed.

Travis took another swallow of whiskey. "Headquarters wants a full report, soon as you're able. An army courier was sent to Monterrey with the information about Colonel Diaz. Word is, he left for the mountains to join the revolution. There's a Major Peters in town who'd like to talk to you. He's in charge of the cavalry they sent down to patrol the river. Peters said they stopped off in Encinal to help with the clean up. Said to tell you and your men that was one hell of a mess you made."

Will drained his glass, and now the bottle was empty. His recollections of the fight were fuzzy with a quart of whiskey in his belly. "They came at us from all sides, Trav. They kept coming. Hadn't seen so much blood since Manassas. I found out I had three good men beside me before that fight was over. I called them saddlebums. Well, they ain't."

Travis made a face. "Be glad you've got 'em, Will. Good men are hard to come by in this country. Let's go across the river and get a bite to eat. I swear that stolen beef tastes better every time I eat it."

Will reached for his crutches and struggled out of his chair, propped on the armrests with a disgusted look on his face. "I never been so tired of anything," he grumbled, hobbling toward the door, swinging his bad leg as he went. "Hand me my hat, Trav. I'm afraid I'll fall over if I reach for it."

They rested after a bountiful meal, cooled by breezes on the little patio at Café Maria. A bowl of fresh limes and a bottle of tequila sat between them. Off in the distance they heard guitars and a woman's voice. The smells of corn tortillas and chilis came from the kitchen.

Travis seemed thoughtfully silent after their meal. He stared at the lights of Nuevo Laredo, toying with his shot glass. "You still aim to turn in your badge, Will?" he asked, ending the silence.

Will shook his head. "Not now. I'd planned to ask Isabella to marry me. Planned to buy a little place and raise a few cows in my old age. I reckon it was just a fool's dream, to think things could work out like I wanted. I figure I'll be wearin' this badge for a while yet . . . till I get too old to climb on a horse."

Travis chuckled. "There's worse things. Like walking behind a plow, or pickin' cotton. Too, a feller has to think about the reason for bein' a Texas Ranger. Ain't many men who can get this job done and live to tell about it. Without the Rangers, men the likes of Zambrano and Hickok have the run of things. There has to be someone to take a side with folks who can't defend themselves. Maybe it's up to men like you and me, Will, to keep things balanced."

Will thought about what Travis said. Some of it made

sense. A man needed a purpose, a reason for what he did to make his living. After a bit Will decided that keeping the balance Travis talked about was reason enough to put his life on the line when it became necessary.

"Here's to the Texas Rangers," Will said, hoisting his glass.

About the Author

Bloody Sunday is Frederic Bean's first book for Fawcett. The author lives in Brownwood, Texas.